SYNOPSIS

Alex lived a peaceful life in the north woods, until she met Paul. His initial considerate behavior disappeared, replaced with inexplicable mood swings, periods of sullen silence and, inevitably, bouts of temper and violence. Then, someone shot him.

The bizarre connections between the suspects unravel a string of deception, apathy, betrayal, and vengeance. Each pathetically humorous character could be labeled victim or perpetrator, but rarely innocent.

These average people chose a path transposing right and wrong and now a series of unlikely events must take place in order to undo each choice.

CHOICE AND CHANCE

To Vicky —
One of my make-believe
" sisters "

Love,
Kris

CHOICE AND CHANCE

Kris Thomsen

To order additional copies of this book, contact:
Xlibris Corporation
1-888-795-4274
www.Xlibris.com
Orders@Xlibris.com
53990

DEDICATION

The book is dedicated to my sisters and my make-believe sisters who
patiently read, listened, enthusiastically encouraged
and unconditionally loved.

Choice And Chance

By Kris Thomsen

"Punishment brings wisdom. It is the healing art of wickedness."
Plato, Gorgias

ALEX

Alex sat on the wrong side of a long metal table in the visitor center of the State Prison. She stared at the neatly folded hands in her lap and instantly recalled the night they held the gun. She knew the long road her mind would travel if she began that journey and yet she could never stop the flow of those repetitious images.

She closed her eyes and Paul's ghostly face wavered as it levitated above his gangly body. The face hung in suspension, then fell, as his tall, thin frame slumped to the floor like a stone gliding through water. She could still hear the ringing in her ears as she fired the single shot that killed him and despite the cold sweat covering her body, she felt a warm flood of relief wash over her knowing he was finally dead.

A hand on her shoulder shocked her to the present. Large brown eyes, inches from her face, returned her questioning look. Alex's gaze drifted down to the guard's enormous breasts. They could have been airbags on a Hummer.

"Alex, you want to go back to your cell?" Bertha asked. "You sure as hell aren't carrying on a conversation and you're acting pretty damn weird."

Alex turned to face her sister's identical worried look. Sydney shook her head slowly, trying to contain the worry and frustration welling inside her. "Damn it, Alex, I feel like you're slipping away from me. You mentally disappear for minutes at a time and the times are increasing. If you don't talk to the attorney tomorrow you'll be praying for God's wrath instead of mine."

Alex grinned, "Floods, pestilence, or famine, Syd? What did you have in mind?"

Their laughter was subdued and hollow, unlike the carefree humor they shared for almost five decades.

Alex returned to her cell to find the door open, a privilege she could enjoy after less than a year. Her cellmate paid for this miniscule amount of freedom with almost five years of her life.

Alex smiled as Jane twirled between their bunks and struck a model's pose. Last week Jane had tediously sewn flags on her sewing duty. This week she drastically altered her uniform so that it clung like an orange skin to her petite 5' 2" body. Her reddish-blond hair hung in long, loose curls that softly framed her face, but her piercing green eyes bore through facial surfaces and Alex could almost feel the curious intrusion in her brain.

Alex exhaled a sigh of contentment when Jane asked about her visit with Sydney. For some reason, the exclusion of daily obligations opened one up to the reality of what was truly important in life. She smiled today for the first time in almost a year because of her sister's unconditional love.

In one year, Jane had become like another sister. Alex felt blessed and yet, Syd's analysis of her bizarre behavior was depressingly accurate. The present simply slipped away as her mind shot to the past with increasing frequency.

Unfortunately, there was no solution to her situation.

2

"Man is the only animal that blushes. Or needs to."
Mark Twain, Puddn'head Wilson's NewCalendar

ALEX

The next day, Alex headed in the direction of the Visitor Center, but she was not expecting the warmth and humor of her sister. She was meeting Victor Morose, the lowest paid, newest addition, to the Sullivan and Mahoney Law Firm, the self-righteous benefactors of the weak and abused.

Alex stared at Victor's too tight, three piece suit, stretching itself over, no more than, 140 pounds of skin and bone. His eagle beaked nose was casting a distinct shadow on his well-worn, white shirt. His overly groomed hair, greased into semi-submission, gave him the look of a cloned hawk. His long, slender fingers were grasping a stack of manila folders and doing a dance up and down the outer edges.

Without sitting, he nervously stuttered, "Mmiss Anderson, yyou haven't been very co-operative."

"I've answered every one of your questions," whispered Alex.

"Then mmaybe I'm not asking the rrright questions. Where did yyou get the gun?"

Alex looked down at her lap and dwelled on that question. She knew she was guilty and confiding in this meek, mild mannered twerp couldn't possibly change the outcome of her future, so why make the attempt.

Her mind wandered to the night she drove to Andy's cabin. She never went out at night, but she had lost all rational thought. Her rage, anger and hurt had become a balloon filled with ridiculous plans for retribution. She was determined to retaliate to Paul's final, horrifying abuse.

Alex knocked on the one-room, cabin door, glanced around the smoke stained walls where small, dead creatures hung and stared fixedly. She blurted out, "What kind of guns do you have, Andy?"

Andy answered her question with a question, "What did you have in mind to kill?"

"The damn raccoon that's been going through my garbage," she replied.

"Got a 357 with shells that could turn him into confetti or a smaller 22, but you'd have to shoot him in the head with that in order to kill him. You don't want him to wander around wounded until he bleeds to death," he warned.

"I don't want to kill him. I just want to scare him. I'll take the .22."

He opened the cabinet, handed her the gun and admonished, "Don't hurt yourself."

Alex loaded the revolver and laid it on the passenger seat. The falling snow severely limited her vision. The driveway had become slick and she fishtailed from one side of the road to the other. Even under these conditions, she could have made the time trials for Daytona as she headed to Paul's house.

"Wwhat did you do wwith the ggun?"

She looked up to see Victor's huge, questioning, brown eyes. They seemed too large for the bony, angular face. Despite the interrogation, they were full of concern and warmth. "Oh God," she thought, "please, don't let me make a connection with another human being. I just can't decipher between your good ones and your bad ones. Why couldn't you make them all good or all evil? It would have made life so easy."

"I really can't remember," Alex murmured.

3

"Why do you rob banks? Because that's where the money is."
Willie Sutton, attributed

ALEX

Alex returned to her cell and when Jane entered, she twirled around to display her latest uniform alteration.

"What do you think?" she grinned. "So what did my little schizophrenic, self-doubting enabler tell that scrawny attorney today? Fat Debbie saw you two and despite desperate attempts at eavesdropping, she got nothing." Jane smiled.

The ten-minute light began blinking and Alex crossed the two feet to the sink, brushed her teeth and climbed into her bunk. Lights went out and the light in her brain switched on, as it did every night.

The vision, that repeated itself for nearly a year, appeared again, like a bad commercial. The crack of a rifle, the sound of glass breaking, the simultaneous explosion of cat hair and down feathers and the blood seeping out of the only breathing roommate Alex had in ten years.

She stood watching the car headlights speed across the frozen lake toward the boat landing and then she crumpled to the floor, hysterically sucking in gulps of air and emitting more than the spent oxygen. There was no point in a trip to the vet for what was lying there.

She heard Paul's voice, the sound of the man she had come to fear over the past two years. "If I really wanted it, you'd be dead. I've already picked off an antelope at 600 yards."

Jane's whisper interrupted her thoughts. "Your sister wants to know why you won't talk to the attorney."

"Because I'm guilty," Alex replied.

"Why'd you shoot him? And don't tell me it's because he shot your cat."

"Why did you embezzle the money?" Alex snapped.

"My employer was the thief. If he hadn't been such a humongous tax evader, the auditor would never have checked the books. That crook should be in here, but he had the money to buy himself out of his little predicament. Now, why did you shoot him?"

Alex opened her eyes and adjusted to the surrounding black. Images began twirling around the ceiling, ghostly forms that had feelings rather than faces. Inadequacy danced by, followed in perfect rhythm by Self-Doubt. A long, thin wisp of pale, blue smoke appeared, Insecurity, arms locked tightly with her friend, Fear, and the tempo accelerated. The whirling emotions, almost suffocating Alex, caused the same dance in the pit of her stomach.

Alex heard her mother's voice warning that people will bring you down faster than you can pick them up, but her mother was referring to alcoholics and drug abusers, not pessimistic control freaks, emotional abusers. Alex never made that distinction.

"Hellooo, I'm waiting," Jane sang.

Alex responded with degradation weighting her voice, "Jane, we're both college graduates from middle class homes and we're in prison. I would say we've made some really bad choices. Now, please go to sleep."

4

"Silence gives consent"
Oliver Goldsmith, The Good Natur'd Man

ALEX

Another visitor. This time it was Sydney. Her big smile slowly faded when she saw Alex.

"You've got to start eating, girl. You're going to make me look bad." They laugh, but then slide into an uncomfortable minute of silence.

"Why won't you open up to him, Alex?"

"Why'd you bother to re-open the case, Syd? I shot the jerk. I mean, I didn't mean to. I aimed over his head, but he's dead. They have the rifle bullet that blew up my cat and they also have my bullet, taken out of Paul. There's a motive there, if you think about it."

"Hang on to your chair, Alex. They took four bullets out of Paul, from two different guns!"

Alex froze in disbelief, her mouth hanging slack, like a child watching a magician.

Sydney stared at her and finally said, "What? It's not as if he was a nice person. I can think of, at least, twenty people who wanted to kill him. Victor didn't want to tell you until we had some hope of finding the guns to match the bullets. You have him so intimidated with your silence that his grade school speech impediment has returned. He wants this case, Alex. It could be his big break in the legal world, but he needs information from you. Please talk to him."

"All I could tell him was that I did it," Alex murmured. "I mean, I aimed over Paul's head, but something must have deflected the bullet. I must have shot him because he slowly sank downward, out of sight."

"Tell him everything you can, Alex. What have we got to lose?"

Alex headed back to her cell where Jane was standing in a thin, gray robe, her shampoo bottle raised over her head.

"You forgot, it's Calgon, take me away time," she quoted.

They shuffled, single file, to the showers and remained in line, semi-relaxed, leaning against walls and lockers. An anorexic looking guard stood across the room with towels draped over her scrawny, crossed arms. She reminded Alex of a carved, cigar store Indian. Her angular face, with its chiseled nose and cheekbones, was motionless, void of any expression that would suggest life and breath.

Alex silently challenged the guard to a competition. Who would give the first indication of motion and human existence?

Alex's vision clouded with steam and surprisingly she pictured herself sinking into a hot, bubble-filled tub, a glass of red wine on the tub's edge and her beautiful cat staring curiously at the water's movement, one small paw batting at bubbles.

"Next, let's go," the guard's smoke damaged, vocal chords, growled. Alex smiled at her miniscule victory. The guard's lips had moved first, but then, she felt the tears on her cheeks and realized they would be ruled as movement.

5

"To know that which lies before us in daily life is the prime wisdom"
John Milton, Paradise Lost

ALEX

Alex returned to her cell and found Jane sitting cross-legged on her bunk with Coke cans and candy wrappers strewn across the blanket. Her metabolism must be over the top of the charts, Alex thought. Beneath the rubble were one and a half sets of five and ten pound barbells. Her left arm was pumping while the right hand shoved the candy bar in her mouth. Then she alternated. The right arm pumped while her left hand held the Coke can to her lips. Alex speculated over the health aspects of minimal prison sports.

"Are you going to talk to the scarecrow attorney?" Jane questioned. "Mindy wants to know. She had another vision last night, some garbage about an angel carrying a rifle."

"Wow, doesn't she ever sleep?" Alex asked.

"Not when her newly adopted flock is roaming. What the heck else has she got to think about, but us, her substitute children?"

Alex recalled her initial fear of Mindy. Her three hundred and fifty pounds rounded the corner of the cell and she stood staring, occasionally licking her lips. Cannibal was the first word that came to Alex. When there was nothing for Mindy to put in her mouth, she would get a glazed look, like a huge, round donut. No one was sure if she was thinking about her lost children or which portion of your torso would taste best.

Alex had the sick thought that if she had known Mindy a year ago; she would have set her on the floor next to Paul's body. Mindy was the ideal garbage disposal.

Alex recalled the first time Paul assaulted her vision. He appeared in the doorway of her office on a hot summer day dressed in white shorts and a white shirt. Heavy gold chains hung around his neck, gold rings circled his fingers and a lumpy, gold watch dangled on his wrist. Her first impression was that of a "pimp" on vacation.

A gangly, underweight frame accentuated his 6'4" height. There was a strong resemblance to Ichabod Crane, but when he spoke his voice was soft and interesting. Perhaps she had misjudged him. Alex was exercising her unfortunate gifts of second-guessing, resulting in her inability to pass judgment.

Alex thought, "Please prove my initial perception wrong. Give every human being the benefit of the doubt." She was dwelling on her past routine of always picking athletic, good-looking men and getting hurt. She convinced herself that it was time to overlook the exterior if the interior was kind and considerate. This time, she would give a nice guy a chance.

"Alex, are you listening?" Jane shattered the vision of Paul into rice-sized satellites and Alex returned.

"Yolanda overheard Mindy telling the shrink that she saw an angel with a rifle standing over your bed. The angel gave you the gun, told you to shoot her ex-husband and she would get her kids back. I guess she forgot that she'd still be in prison and hardly an attentive mother. I swear she's getting worse under all of this professional care."

Jane giggled and said, "Looks like you've got a new profession, Alex; killing people."

"Stop it, Jane, I just lost it, but I had no intention of killing him. I felt as though my head was filling with helium for months. I had constant headaches and pain in my stomach. The intensity of the arguments with Paul was growing like some creepy tumor. Our levels of anger rose so far above any sort of communication level that my body would heat up to a boiling point within seconds." Alex paused and then added despondently, "You know what's pathetic? The feelings I had were those associated with what I always considered 'low-class' people. I could picture them in their stinking, walk-up tenement slum dwellings, screaming foul abuses. Their impatience for each other's shortcomings always resulted in violence."

Jane did not get the connection.

Alex finally looked up, eyes glistening, "I had become one of them, a real troll. I resented Paul for bringing me to his level. I allowed him into my life and somehow gave him permission to bring me to that humiliating point in my life. I guess people live that way out of desperation or they don't know any better. I did know better and I had to get out. It took a couple of years, Jane, before the explosives went off in my head." There was an unnerving silence before Alex blurted, "You don't just shoot people."

6

"Things are always at their best in their beginning."
Pascal, Provincial Letters

ALEX

Alex stretched out on the bed and was surprised to see her hipbones protruding from beneath her T-shirt. She assumed the sleepless nights were taking their toll. The lack of sleep was consuming the nutrition from the only cooking in the world she considered inferior to hers.

This would be another chart buster on the Insomniac's Hit Parade.

The thought that there might be a "God's Plan" slowly mushroomed like a nuclear cloud in her head. It had to be God's plan, because there must be a reason for a moron like Paul to have entered her little world, a darn good reason, she just didn't have it.

Six months after Paul's first visit to her office, he reappeared. She studied the tall "toothpick," his thick blond, permed hair, the Mr. "T" jewelry and a smile that revealed slightly crooked teeth. Once again, she thought, no one could look like this and have so much self-confidence, unless he was a truly good person.

Paul had just passed the state exam for an appraiser's license and wanted to obtain the necessary hours of experience. Her boss, David, hired him and the slick, muddy, landslide began its slimy decent. The office was extremely busy, but despite the workload, Alex had time to observe some serious mood swings in Paul. She chalked these up to home problems, since work was not very stressful; if you disregarded David's frequent temper tantrums and his obsessive, compulsive interest in lawsuits and legal issues.

David was a short, scrawny, little man with a "Napoleon" complex. His dark hair, cut in an early "Beatles" style, flopped like a mop when he walked and his little feet pointed outward in a duck imitation; the way heavyweight people walk, as if they needed additional stability. In David's case, he probably needed that stance to support the gigantic ego, swelling in his tiny, peanut-shaped, head.

The tension between Paul and David escalated over the next six months, until it stretched across the office like a tightrope. Alex kept waiting for one of the performers to lose their balance and crash to the big top's floor, bypassing the safety net. She had reached a point where it didn't matter which ropewalker fell, she just wanted the tension to end.

Alex kept thinking about leaving David and working at home and very coincidentally, Paul decided he was also leaving. He suggested they start their own office.

"They shoot horses, don't they?"

7

_____

"Better sleep with a sober cannibal than a drunken Christian."
Herman Melville, Moby Dick

ALEX and PAUL

They began doing inspections together after Alex almost slid off a thirty-foot cliff. She snow-shoed to a seasonal cabin and then realized that the three feet of snow, shoveled from the roof, was now solid ice all the way around the house. She had to measure the exterior so she shimmied up the icy slope like an aging Spider Woman. Thirty seconds later, she was hanging from a tree branch trying not to imagine the sickening sound of breaking bones when she eventually hit the frozen lake.

She arrived back at the office looking like she had been "gang-raped." The ice cuts and branch scrapes ran from her waist to her shoulders, her coat was torn and her eyes were frozen in huge, dark circles that contrasted sharply with her chalky, white face.

Paul insisted that he accompany her on inspections the next day.

"What made you move to northern Minnesota?" Paul asked.

"Actually, it was my old boyfriend. He was the World Champion of socializers and after eight years of partying in almost every city on the globe, I chanced on the idea that living in the worst available climate would reduce the social circle."

"What did the old boyfriend think about that move?"

"Not happy and I felt sick about leaving. He was a dynamite person. One of those few people in life who created a career that revolves around his best-loved interests. His career became his life and his wife. I just didn't fit in. I needed more privacy and 'down time', but if he ever needed me . . . . Can't live with him, but never want to be without him in my life."

Paul was quiet, digesting her response and then suggested they stop for something to eat.

They entered a typical, northern extremities tavern and saw the sullen owner drinking at the other end of the bar.

"Yeah, what'll it be?" He reluctantly interrupted his own happy hour.

Alex gazed around at the heads of deer, elk, antelope and monstrous fish that hung on the walls. There were more stuffed animals in that place than at Toys 'R Us.

Alex got the uneasy feeling that the creatures were staring at her. Well, she decided, they would have to wait their turn. When the bartender finished, they would get their chance.

"You from around here?"

Paul replied, "We have an office in Medicine Lake."

"Sure could have fooled me," he slurred.

Alex glanced at Paul and his red hat, red coat and gold chains exploded in her vision. I bet the bartender thought he was an unemployed Santa, rushing the season and then she wondered, "Who do you know that has the self confidence or ego to sport such radical garb?"

"You know, I'm not sure I like the idea of this Mr. Social in your life. I mean an "ex" is an "ex." I would kill mine, if I thought I could get away with it.

"He's not really in my life anymore, Paul. I couldn't live his life style, but that doesn't mean I didn't love him," Alex explained.

Paul's eyes narrowed to slits, he turned his back on Alex and began a conversation with four men on his other side. They were discussing ammunition size, guns, "points" on "racks" and things that go "bump in the night." Alex had just crossed into the "Twilight Zone."

These were conversations where you leave "the little woman" at home, yet there she was, in another bar, similar to the hundreds she had frequented with Mr. Social. The fact that this bar was not associated with a Yacht Club was the only real difference.

Alex couldn't pinpoint when she began losing control over her life again. It was happening too fast.

It became routine to stop for a drink every time they finished their inspections. After a year, they had stopped at almost every tavern and restaurant in an eighty-mile radius. Paul always helped Alex with her coat, opened doors, feigned interest in her conversation and ate rather graciously, as opposed to the clamorous, lip smacking, open-mouthed chewing she now endured at the office.

"What do you do the other six evenings, when we're not out on inspections?" Paul asked.

Alex didn't even have to ponder her exact routine, she replied instantly. "I pour a glass of wine, call my sisters, play with my cat, read my mail, cook my dinner, have another glass of wine and usually an after dinner cocktail. Then I brush my teeth and go to bed.

I have the same drinks every night, but no more than that or God sends me one of those 'Killer' hangovers that I didn't believe existed when I was in college," Alex laughed.

That must have been the golden gift of weakness to play upon, because from then on, every stop they made dragged into a marathon.

"How about one more," Paul would ask and three seconds after the decline, "How about now?" Or he would just order another one while Alex was in the restroom.

One evening, as they finished dinner, Alex began to feel anxious, as if this one, particular step into Paul's social world might be quicksand. She glanced around the room, ablaze with neon orange; pants, jackets, suspenders, and hats that were still on heads at dinner tables. She flashed back to her "movie addict" years and scenes from "Fargo" came to life.

Alex knew many women, in this northern climate, who held at least one job, usually two. The men carve ducks and decoys or guide for hunters or anglers on a seasonal basis. The phrase, "I'm a real go-getter" means they go and get their wives from all of their different jobs. These women made Clydesdales look like Shetland ponies. This environment might not be the one Alex would select as permanent. That sudden realization fertilized her growing confusion and she ordered another drink.

She slammed the Manhattan and Paul quickly ordered another. He provoked meaningless conversation and a fourth Manhattan waived before her eyes, like a phony mirage in a steaming desert.

They sat in her driveway with her house growing larger, then, shrinking, until Alex crunched one eye closed to control the movement. Paul reached across the seat and began massaging her neck and shoulders. Her last vision was Paul in too-tight Jockeys leaning over her bed, breathing heavily and shooing her cat away.

Alex awoke with a heavy fuzziness, queasy stomach and a piercing pain below her right eye. The classic symptoms of the customary hangovers attributed to her last relationship with Mr. Social. Her cat was next to her head, staring at her with an accusing expression that clearly indicated displeasure over her incredible "screw up," and Alex wondered if she should take that look literally.

Paul was gone, no note, no traces of underwear or discarded socks. "Oh, please God, let this be a huge nightmare," she pleaded, but then her mind began twirling in small circles of fear and distrust. If what she thought happened, wouldn't you at least leave a note explaining your departure? Alex always had an aversion to sneaky people and a warning wave rolled through her stomach. Something was very creepy about Paul.

She was in a Stage 5 of aftershock. What had she done? Her head had been so far up her butt she could have done her own colonoscopy.

8

ALEX

"Don't you think Paul and David had some serious issues going on between them?" Sydney asked.

"I guess David had some issues with me, too, after the way we left his employment, but then, David had issues with everyone," Alex shrugged.

She hugged herself and started rocking back and forth, as she recalled the afternoon of the confrontation.

Knowing they still had to pick up their computers and file cabinets from David dampened the excitement of moving to their new office.

Paul dropped Alex off to pick up her car and left. By the time Alex reached David's, she could hear shouting from the street and when she stepped inside they were squared-off, inches from each other's face. David told Paul that all of their appraisals belonged to him.

Vulgar, abusive words were trailing through Paul's tightly pinched lips.

Alex stepped forward to remind David that those files had to remain with the appraiser that did them, for a minimum of five years.

Paul pushed her backward and his voice had risen so high that his next insults came out sounding like a tiny girl, except, a small girl could not have possibly known that many filthy, slang words for various body parts.

Alex was feeling light-headed and out of touch with reality. She thought, "This couldn't be happening between educated adults" and suddenly remembered, neither David nor Paul had much education, "Out of the frying pan and into the fire."

They emerged with their computers and some files, loaded the car and drove in silence for a few miles.

Alex was shaking and her stomach felt as if five-scale tremors were rolling with occasional volcanic eruptions.

"You didn't have to lose control like that. We could have reasoned with David," she whispered.

"Shut the fuck up, and don't ever question my actions in front of anyone again. You understand?"

They remained in silence for the rest of the drive and an additional week afterwards.

"Al-ex," Sydney droned. "Are you listening? Where do you go when we're talking?"

Alex turned to Syd. "I think about all the tell-tale signs that led me to my new environment."

"Well, try to remember all of those details when you talk to Victor. He's almost positive he can reverse your sentence and get you out of this environment. It all depends on what you can remember."

Alex returned to her cell to find Jane facing the wall. There were tissues all over her bed and muffled moans.

Wwhat's wrong?" Alex stammered.

"They found Mindy, hanging in the laundry room. Oh Alex, I only have three weeks to go and I don't think I can make it. This place is creeping me out. She had a picture of an angel pinned to her uniform. What the hell is that supposed to mean? I mean, what the hell is that? She sees the shrink twice a week. None of this is working. There's no hope for any of us and as much as I hate it in here, getting out is even scarier. What will I do? Who's going to hire me? I'll probably end up just like Mindy."

Jane broke into sobs that sounded like hiccups. Alex sat next to her, put her arm around her shoulder and they just rocked. When the waves of sobs subsided, Alex told her, "I have a plan."

That night, a plan came to Alex. She thought out-loud, "You know, God, despite the stupid choices you let me make, I don't believe you ever left my side. I have great friends, great sisters and even though none of my relationships lasted for a lifetime, they were interesting and, I guess, educational. I just wish I could have all the years back that I wasted, following some else's interests and never taking the time to develop my own."

9

"Public opinion is always in advance of the law."
John Galsworthy, Windows

JAKE

Scrawny Victor raced through the doorway, looking like an elf passing through a castle gate. His new haircut looked like the crown on a parakeet, rather than a hawk. His bony knees protruded from his well-worn suit pants with each giant step he took. He was anxiously striding across the glossy, vinyl floor.

"I have ggood news. Your sister, Syd, gave us a list of the people you thought might have had a motive and your former employer, David, is right at the top. It seems David and Paul had a very vocal argument in front of several people at the Courthouse just a few days before Paul's death. Jake is questioning everyone that saw the disagreement."

"Jake?" Alex questioned.

"My rright arm," he beams. "We've been friends since college. He passed the bar, but preferred the detective end, the chase. He puts it all together."

The acrylic door slid open and it framed an incredible hulk. Now, it looked like the entire castle was passing through the gate. Jake loomed, inches from the header, feigned a moderate duck and a huge grin filled the lower half of his head, revealing straight, white teeth in a tanned face.

He crossed the entire room in four strides, held out his hand and beamed, "You must be the reason for Vic's latest crusade."

Alex could not help but smile back. In fact, she actually chuckled as she said, "Nice to meet you." From the moment of Jake's entrance, Victor's stuttering ceased.

Jake was radiating success. "You know," he said in a voice that sounded as if it were coming out of a deep well. "When the police first searched your office they were trying to find out everything about you, since you were their number one suspect. This time we went in looking for Paul's records and Bingo. That son of a gun had dirt on everyone, but more importantly, he was creating his own dirt. From his records, we found eleven law-suits pending and at least two dozen complaints filed on two different people. This led our suspicions to his home records and, another Bingo. That correspondence revealed several written requests to the IRS to investigate his wife's tax returns. We'll be questioning her soon."

"Now, back to you." Victor's large brown eyes, fixed on Alex.

She explained that she had hunted grouse and done some trap shooting; she was not a novice with guns and could not believe that she had shot Paul. She may have accidentally grazed him, at the very worst. Still, he did fall to the floor after her shot.

"Who arrested you and what did you tell them?" urged Jake.

"It was the local deputy, Stuart something, and I couldn't talk at all. I was sort of frozen." Alex grew distant, as though she were "time-traveling."

She stood at the window in her bedroom watching the sheriff's car speed up her driveway. The red and blue lights were twirling. She had another flashback to her movie years, but this was no screenplay and she reacted in a rigid imitation of a cryogenic experiment, gone bad. She slowly, stiffly maneuvered to her door and became transfixed on the red and blue reflections spinning off the snow covered house, cottage and trees.

The thin, red headed deputy had his hand on his holster and asked for Alexandra Anderson. Me, she thought, the little freezer-burned experiment, who stared vacantly out of sleepless, sunken sockets. If she could have blocked out Stuart's high-pitched voice, with its slight lisp, reading her rights, the colors dancing around the trees and snow were quite beautiful, like an early Christmas present.

Alex returned from the haunting memory to find Vic and Jake gaping incredulously. "Had she spoken all of that out loud?" she wondered. "Oh God," she prayed, "Please don't let me be crazy." She silently reprimanded herself, "How could I have thought I could play Paul's games? His games were never part of my environmental or moral background."

"They will drag you down to their level," her mother's voice repeated.

10

ALEX

Another buzzer sounded, like an echo in the distance. The sound shrunk itself, entered Alex's ear and she awoke to the confining space of the cell. Jane's legs swung down over the top bunk as she counted, "14, 13, 12, 11, 10, oh shit, nine days and I'm back on the unpredictable streets, surrounded by crazies in a deteriorating society."

"I told you, Jane, I've got a plan, possible employment and security for you," Alex smiled.

"Could you, like, share this with me before the stress reaches my heart?" Jane did not smile.

"Everything will be finalized after I meet with Syd today. I'll fill you in tonight, OK?"

They headed down to the Breakfast of Champions and surrounded themselves within the protective circle of the few people that might not stab, wound or eat them. Everyone was relatively subdued since Mindy's demise. Inwardly, they were all afraid of slipping through the same humungous cracks in the system.

They separated, Jane headed to the sewing room, Alex in the direction of her sister and a semblance of the organized, routine past.

When Alex sat down at the table, there was a pressing, ominous veil of defeat pressing its weight upon them.

"What?" Alex provoked.

"Jake tried to talk to Pat and she threw him out. She said the divorce was over, she had no clue as to what happened to Paul, and if Jake came around again, she'd sue for harassment. He doesn't have enough evidence to bring her in for additional questioning, to file a search warrant, nothing. He didn't think she'd react with this much hostility. He thought, even an ex-wife would want to know what caused her husband's death."

"Oh no, I asked him not to question her yet, now she'll be overly cautious and defensive. I need your help, Syd. We're going to need money. Please call the Realtor who sold me my house. She always said she had several buyers waiting for any house on my lake. In the meantime, I'll call my banker and borrow against the house. I have to get money for Jane. She needs to be able to work and no employer can refuse Jane's charm combined with weak demands for less than minimal wages.

"Oh Alex, you love your house. We can hang on a little longer."

"If this doesn't happen, Syd, I'll be in here for so long, I won't need a house. I'm starting to believe that I really didn't kill Paul."

When Alex entered the sewing room, Jane was perched nervously on the edge of a chair. She whispered, "Alex, share your damn plan with me before I need to buy stock in 'Depends'."

They returned to their cell and whispered until long after lights out. Jane was giggling at the prospect of such an enormous charade. Enthusiasm for a game of wits, deception and justice replaced her fear of struggling back into the declining western civilization.

Alex could not have found a more receptive partner and yet, the fear of another stupid game loomed darkly in her mind. She remained with her eyes glued open until dawn. She held her thin, scratchy blanket close to her face for security.

11

"Happy families are all alike;
every unhappy family is unhappy in its own way"
Leo Tolstoy, Anna Karenina

The JUDGE

Judge Manning's eyes opened to the early dawn sun and he felt the smoothness of silk on his cheek. The remainder of the sheet slid off during the night and he realized his entire body was uncovered. "Damn sheets," he muttered and gazed toward the bathroom where his wife was soaking in a French oil bath. "My lazy daughter is probably soaking in the same stuff," he muttered again.

"Clare, what time is my first appointment?" He called.

"Darling, do I look like your secretary?" Her disinterested response annoyed him.

"I'll be lucky if Jennifer and I make it to the benefit brunch in a timely fashion. Could you hurry over to her room and make sure she's dressing?"

The Judge walked the length of the long hallway and knocked on Jenny's door. No response. He knocked again and when silence followed the knock, he slowly turned the handle, unprepared for the sour smell of stale liquor and marijuana that slipped through the cracked doorway.

"God, Jenny, open some windows in here before you die from these second-hand fumes. As he made his way to the window, the thought that she had already inhaled first-hand fumes tickled his temper. This was always the way it started whenever he got near his daughter. There she was, sprawled on the king-sized bed in the same clothes she had gone out in, the night before. Or, lack of them, he noted.

He scrutinized the short, jean cut-offs that exposed a third of Jenny's butt, a string tied swim suit top that was no longer holding in either ample breast and the many silver bracelets surrounding both ankles in a mock version of prison chains. "She'll probably end up in those," he thought angrily.

When she didn't stir after he flung the drapes and banged windows open, he leaned over and touched her shoulder.

She jumped to a sitting position with a small raised fist. When she focused on her father, she blurted, "What the hell do you want?"

"Your mother wants you to get dressed for some benefit you're supposed to attend."

"Up hers, I don't feel good."

"You don't feel well," the Judge, corrected.

"Well, up yours too, daddy, now get out. I'm tired."

"I won't tolerate this behavior anymore, Jenny. Get up and get dressed," he warned.

"Or what, you'll beat me up? You'll arrest me? You'll haul me in front of that 'joke court' of yours? Go kiss momma's big butt."

The Judge spun towards the door stifling the urge to slap her defiant, little face. When he reached his bedroom, he shouted to Clare, "I'm not doing this anymore. You've let her run rampant and I can no longer be responsible for her behavior."

"Oh dear," Clare wheezed, while she strained to zip the colorful caftan she had selected. "She's really a very good girl, dear. She's just a little mixed up in these puberty years and all the women at my club rave about how beautiful she is."

"Clare, you talk about her like she's a show dog in the International Kennel Club. She's a child and needs discipline."

"She'll grow through this stage, darling. Have patience."

"Clare, she's been up before my bench three times. I can't overlook anymore of her wrong doings. I can't bail her out of her predicaments anymore," the Judge emphasized his statement with a fist on the dresser.

"Darling, please. Oh, and before you leave, stop in the kitchen and have the cook prepare lamb chops for our little get-together tonight. She'll coordinate the rest of the menu."

The Judge stared hard at the woman he had married twenty-four years earlier and was actually surprised that he hardly knew her anymore. They slept in different rooms, entertained strangers nightly, and neither had any idea of what each other did during a normal day.

He strode toward the shower and once the hot water revitalized his aching body, he categorized the marital changes that led to his present state of anger, resentment, frustration and basic total misery.

When he was a struggling young attorney, they had mutual interests and friends, but when more money came in, Clare discovered new ways to spend it, always outdoing her last social event. She developed an obnoxious, nasal twang and began boasting about academic accomplishments that belied her single year of college.

When they conceived Jenny, six years into their marriage, (despite the consistent, but seldom-needed use of birth control) Clare's entire personality changed. She became whiny and unbelievably demanding, as if the entire pregnancy was his fault. She had a new wing added to the house, with her new bedroom separated from his, by the nursery. The screams and cries during the night went unattended by Clare and the Judge approached his bench with little more than three hours sleep each night for almost two years.

Clare, later, redecorated the nursery into a guest room, an exercise room and eventually an office. She added another new wing for their six-year old daughter's continual banishment. Clare renewed her demanding social life and maintained minimum contact with her daughter until she turned thirteen. It was, finally, time to display her beautiful, little accomplishment.

The Judge stepped from the shower and tried to stop thinking about their disintegrating marriage. He promptly dressed and hurriedly left the house, hoping to avoid both of them.

12

"It has long been an axiom of mine that the little things
are infinitely the most important."
A. Conan Doyle,
A Case of Identity in the Adventures Of Sherlock Holmes

ALEX

Alex was miserable. Jake and Victor were waiting in the visitor center when she made her disappointing appearance. There were heavy, puffy bags accented by dark circles below her eyes from the continuous deprivation of sleep.

Vic broke the silence. "Sydney told us what you're trying to do and it's stupid. Jane was released less than a week ago and you're setting her up to get killed. She doesn't know what she's getting into. Paul's ex-wife is no fool.

"Do you have a better idea?" Alex asked.

Jake cautioned, "Patience, we'll work on Pat."

"I'll be ninety-five with no chance of parole. No thanks. Please, just give Jane a couple of weeks. She's no fool either and besides, if the police show up again, Pat will really be suspicious. Right now, she knows I've been found guilty and she's feeling relatively safe."

"Sydney told us that would be your reply, so, here are some of things Jane has to get."

"We need copies of Pat's correspondence with Paul, copies of correspondence with attorneys relating to Paul's accusations and any information regarding the IRS. We need to know if she's experienced with guns and if she owns one, and it wouldn't hurt to get some inside scoop on her feelings toward Paul. Maybe Jane could record their conversations."

"Jeepers, why don't you just ask Jane to sleep with her?"

"We told you your logic was beyond absurd. If Pat had anything to do with Paul's death, she could be extremely dangerous."

"Jane knows that and she still wants to do it," Alex offered weakly.

"Loyalty to her friend and ignorance of danger, that's a great combination. You suppose Harry Potter and his wizard friends might save Jane?" scolded Vic. Jake stood towering over her chair with a similar scowl on his face.

"Please, let us try. If it gets weird or scary, Jane promises to come back and we'll work on Plan B." Alex was begging.

Victor sat down next to her. Softly, he said, "Have you given anymore thought as to what might have happened to the gun you had that night?"

"I have," Alex murmured, "but nothing is coming to me except a vision of myself in my car with my face in my hands, crying. It couldn't have been with me in my car 'cause my hands were free. I must have dropped it between Paul's house and my car."

"We searched the grounds around his house three times. Nothing. The only gun the police found was inside the house. A .38 that belonged to Paul. His fingerprints were on it and the safety was off, which struck me somewhat funny. I mean, he had a stockpile of guns and a license to sell arms. Someone with that much exposure to weapons is unlikely to leave a gun lying around that's ready to fire." Jake shook his head negatively and said, "Keep trying to remember, Alex. We'll be back tomorrow afternoon."

13

"Alas! How difficult it is not to betray our guilt by our countenance."
Ovid, Metamorphoses

The JUDGE

The Judge did not sleep at all that night. He replayed the boring dinner conversation and visualized Jenny's pouting face directed toward her plate for over an hour. That dinner was enough to drive him to drink. He could see how an eighteen-year old would prefer a drunken state of mind as opposed to listening to an over-the-hill, untalented actor from one of Clare's local theater groups. If the imbecile had offered one more, inept recitation from Shakespeare, the Judge would have crawled over the table and cut off the fool's oxygen.

He watched Clare's rapacious tongue darting in and out of her mouth with equal greed for both the food and gossip. His stomach began churning with disgust and he tore his thoughts from the dinner group and directed them to his court cases.

Judge Burke had recently passed away and Judge Simmons took early retirement due to health problems. The Governor had not appointed replacements. Judge Manning was not only carrying his normal calendar, but also hearing appeals.

His daughter was back in court that morning on drug possession charges. The Judge disregarded all evidence and pronounced probation and community service. Shortly after her hearing, a sixteen-year old boy, also charged with drug possession, entered the courtroom. The Judge's mind remained focused on his daughter and he sentenced the boy to two years in Juvenile Detention. It would be a screaming miracle if he were re-elected after that farce.

His mind remained on his spoiled daughter and his life; a life that consisted of trivial dinner parties, mundane conversation, lack of emotional affection and a major lack of sleep.

A middle-aged, brunette, sentenced to fifty years in prison for murder, entered the courtroom, but his circle of concentration wound too tightly around his daughter. He only scanned her appellate lawyer's written brief, which argued that the police did not find a weapon and there were no witnesses. It also contained the fact that the results from an autopsy were unavailable until after the trial, but the Judge was preoccupied and did not take enough time to read that far.

He could only see her dark hair as she sat, quietly crying. The assistant district attorney sharply interjected that he had a signed confession from Alex something or other.

The Judge never even saw her face. "We have a signed confession and I have reviewed all of the trial court's proceedings and I affirm the judgment of the District Court. The Judge banged his gavel, retreated to his chambers and removed his robe. He was dreading the confrontation he was about to engage in with Jenny.

Alex might as well have been an alien. She was non-existent on that particular day in the Judge's world. Today another face haunted his memory.

Over three years ago, a tall, Afro-American woman entered his court with her appointed attorney. Jenny had not been home in three days and the Judge hadn't slept for the same amount of time. She had gone out of the house several times in the past month dressed like a Hollywood whore. This time, he couldn't ignore it. Jenny's hair was dyed the pink and blue colors he had become used to. It stood six inches straight up the center of her head. When she turned to close the door, the Judge noticed a large, silver ring piercing her upper lip. The vision of that black girl in his courtroom flashed before his eyes. She had that huge zipper-like scar running down the side of her face and it sent a tingling chill down his back. She had not chosen that scar. Some savage left that indelible signature.

Now, his stupid daughter was marking up her perfect body with hideous, self-inflicted wounds. He lost his temper and hadn't seen her for days. While he pondered Jenny's whereabouts, he nonchalantly sentenced that black woman to life imprisonment for the murder of her husband.

He had no recollection of how she reacted, because he had tuned out. There were statements signed by doctors and nurses he never read. There were photographs that he never looked at. His mind had been on his spoiled daughter and his empty life.

Now, he wondered if that woman's husband might have stolen some of her high cheek-boned beauty and caused enough pain and suffering to warrant a lesser sentence.

14

"If you can't say anything good about someone, sit right here by me"
Alice Roosevelt Longworth, The New York Times

JAKE

Jake smiled at Alex as he strode across the visitor floor. "Vic couldn't make it; he's tied up in court."

"Let's get down to the night of Paul's death, Alex."

Every sleepless night had become that night for Alex. She closed her eyes and described the constant scene that played in the darkness of her cell.

"Well, there were two cars parked to the right, away from the house. Paul's snowplow was one of them, but I didn't really look at the second one. I was too upset and confused to care."

"What was weird was that Paul opened the inside door with his left hand, you know, awkwardly crossing his body. His right arm just hung there and his face was a ghastly white, not his usual, reddish, high blood pressure look. There were ketchup stains all over his shoulder and a crazy thought went through my head, even his slovenly eating habits couldn't have spread that far."

"He didn't look scared, which was all I wanted. Instead, he looked unbelievably angry, as if I had already assaulted him. He raised his left arm and extended his middle finger against the glass, inches from my face.

I aimed the gun to the right of his head, above his shoulder and pulled the trigger. I felt defiant and yelled, 'that's for my cat,' but then he slowly dropped to the floor and I couldn't believe it. I panicked and ran for my car."

"Can you think of anyone that might have wanted Paul dead?"

"Well, he had a finger-in-the-chest, poking contest with one of the local, shyster Realtors," Alex offered and Jake smiled.

"If that guy was less than honest, it's probably a routine confrontation for him, not a murderous, revenge motive. Alex, I'm talking real anger, think."

"OK, maybe David. They were archenemies since our less than cordial departure. And, maybe Paul's ex-wife. He totally hated her and would not get over it. We would be on inspections and he would tell people that his divorce took eight years, but he was getting even."

"Alright, it's worth some phone calls and footwork," Jake said.

"Jake, I really think it was me he hated the most. Two years ago, Paul told me he tore up his wife's credit cards. He told her she was too stupid to use them responsibly. One day we were leaving my driveway and I brought up what was bothering me. Paul went out every night and his favorite bars were 20-30 miles away. He drove out west a couple times a year, down to Minneapolis a couple times a month and to southern Minnesota to visit his family weekly. I never went out and never drove anywhere except to and from work."

Alex said, "I mentioned to Paul that I thought, maybe, we should get separate business credit cards for gasoline and I explained to him what I just told you. My body slammed into the dashboard at the same time I heard the screech of brakes. He pulled out his wallet and threw the credit card in my face. He hissed at me like a snake, 'You and my ex, always this damn, get-even shit, I could kill you both.'"

Jake shook his head, reached across the table and lifted Alex's chin. "Girl, you may truly be the wimp of the world. Every time you speak up for what's right, you get hurt. Paul didn't hate you the most. You rejected him, just like his wife and he was substituting you for her. You were calling him on shots that he thought he had scored against her. This game isn't over, yet."

15

"While we have prisons, it matters little which of us occupies the cells."
George Bernard Shaw,
Maxims for Revolutions in Man and Superman

ALEX

Alex glanced at her calendar and according to the X's, it was Saturday, a day she used to treasure. She would set her alarm clock just so she could shut it off and sink back into deep dreams. She quickly jumped out of her bunk when she realized she was on kitchen duty today and would be scrubbing pots and pans until, at least, noon.

As she was returning to her cell, Bertha told her she had a call. She gave Alex a slight smile and nod, as if they were sharing a secret. Alex picked up the receiver and waited for the call to pass the switchboard. A familiar voice sang, "Alex, you old convict, what's shakin'?"

"Jane?" Alex giggled. "Where the heck are you?"

"I'm standing in the middle of my new living room, in my new apartment, in a new neighborhood and I've sewn some new clothes. I can promise you, they aren't orange." There was a moment of silence.

"Alex?" She recognized her sister's voice.

"Syd, what the heck are you doing, wherever you are?"

"I couldn't let Jane do this alone and as much as I love him, I needed a break from the man I so fervently prayed for. I think he was as happy about my vacation as I was," she laughed and there was another moment of silence.

"Alex, I know you don't have much time." Jane was back. "Here's the gist. I am in. I have a job in one of her Minneapolis health clubs. Haven't met her yet, but it is going to happen. Here's the number you can reach me at and Jake is coming tomorrow to fill me in on the right moves." Did I ever tell you your sister is a lot more fun than you are? She says you used to be fun and I can't wait to see that side of you." A guard with a one-minute warning interrupted them.

"Alex, you've got a lot of good friends and we're going to get you out."

"I miss you, Jane. The old cell just isn't home anymore, without you." The phone went dead before Alex finished her sentence.

That night Bertha opened Alex's cell door and gently pushed in a thin, mousy looking girl.

"This here's Shirley and she don't talk," Bertha attempted a pathetic smile.

Alex stood staring at the girl while sizing up her gangly frame. Her wrists were the size of Alex's fingers. Her mousy brown hair was thin and straggly. Her pasty complexion had fine, blue lines running through it, like messed up road maps. The girl had huge brown eyes that not only dwarfed her face, but made her whole body seem out of proportion. Her skinny arms wrapped around her body as if she was hiding something or maybe missing a doll that was once there. Where in hell do these girls come from and what horrible things happened in their lives to bring them to this condition? Alex was thinking she might be another Mindy and she wondered if this one would talk to the shrink. Would the shrink bring her to the same end?

Alex told her to hop up to Jane's old bunk and asked if she needed another blanket. There was total silence as she climbed up, got in and turned towards the wall. Alex couldn't even hear her breathe. The walking dead, she thought.

The lights went out and Alex pulled the blanket up to her eyes. They would probably remain open all night to watch over the new creature in her home.

16

"Everything is dangerous, my dear fellow.
If it wasn't so, life wouldn't be worth living."
Oscar Wilde, The Importance of Being Earnest

JANE

She was working into her eleventh-hour at the health club, with no overtime. She thought about Alex and wondered if she would ever meet Paul's "ex." It had been two weeks of ten-hour days and Pat had not checked on this club once. She had to keep an eye on these clubs or she wouldn't be so successful, Jane thought, and then debated over quitting this one and working at a different club. Maybe they don't rehire after someone quits.

Her mind raced and suddenly the side door opened and a tall, good-looking, blond glided through the door with an expensive white coat that swirled around very shapely legs. She looked like a model and when she flashed her white smile, Jane could not help but respond with her own. They shook hands and made a connection.

"So, you're the workaholic," she smiled. "I thought I'd give you a little more time. Many of the girls start like you for a few days and then burn out. This time, I think I have a 'keeper.' You remind me of myself when I first got into the business. I knew I would never make it working for someone else, so I put in the extra hours, earned a management position, increased my salary and squirreled it away to lease my first club. I needed to succeed in order to get away from my asshole husband. What's your motivating force?"

"I created my own personal bad luck and I'm trying to reverse the situation."

"Glad you brought that up and glad you're taking the responsibility. I had you checked out and I personally frown on embezzling, particularly from my own business," she laughed. "Well, I'm out of here. Nice meeting you and keep up the good work." She glided toward the door, then turned and flashed one more smile, "By the way, you've just earned your first pay increase. It starts today."

The door closed and Jane stood staring, as if Pat was still in the room. "Boy," Jane thought, "I sort of hope she didn't shoot Paul. I think I like her."

Jane locked up and drove back to her apartment. Syd had dinner waiting and an unfamiliar sense of security warmed Jane. She began chattering about the meeting and admitted to liking Pat. Syd grinned, "What's not to like? She had to be a saint to stay married to that flaming ass, Paul, for twenty years."

The next day Jane was working out with a new member and she had a real rush of job security as she watched the big, white, fleshy arms struggle with a five-pound weight. "Lifetime Membership" flashed in her brain.

The side door flew open and Pat whirled through in black leather pants, cropped, leather jacket, and a white sweater accented with a tasteful black and tan scarf. A black leather beret emphasized her highlighted blond hair. She looked awesome.

"I'm trying to squeeze in lunch today. Want to join me?"

They got into Pat's Jaguar and drove a few blocks to an exclusive looking restaurant. They were only half way through eating when Pat said, "Jane, I'm having problems at my Westfield Club. I have to fire the manager and I need you to fill in. If it gets back on track, you would keep the management position."

Jane was ecstatic. She thought of a new career in the making and then suddenly remembered Alex. If what they suspected came true, her career would be short-lived.

"Do I detect some hesitation?" asked Pat.

"No, no, I have the time, the energy and I sure could use the extra money. Thank you."

"Your records indicate a name change. Divorced?" Pat asks.

"He couldn't face his friends or family when I was convicted. He had to leave me." Jane responds.

"Right," Pat murmurs, "For better or for worse."

"Have you ever been married?" Jane asked, "And feel free to tell me to mind my own business."

"I'm married to an older man who has become my best friend and confidant. He is wonderful. He's patient with my business hours and great with my daughter. What a switch from her real father." Pat looked down and Jane could feel that she was far away in that moment.

When Pat looked up again, her smile returned and she said, "Well, that was all very long ago and very over with."

Pat dropped Jane back at the health club and roared away in her beautiful car.

17

"The robbed that smiles steals something from the thief"
Shakespeare, Othello

JANE

The Westfield Club was twice the size of the one Jane left. There were only four more instructors and almost double the members. Her first impression was, "Whoa, we're understaffed." This was not going to be as easy as she thought, she could be fired and out of the information loop in a week.

On the second day, Pat showed up, but went straight to the office. Jane locked up at closing time without seeing Pat leave. This went on for four more days and finally Jane's curiosity overcame her caution.

She thought of a weak excuse to enter the office and found Pat huddled next to an elderly woman with tightly braided hair piled on the top of her head like a gray turd.

They appeared to be "cooking the books" and Jane made a feeble joke to that effect. Pat glared up at her, "We're being audited, again. This is the fourth time in four years, thanks to my ex-husband. I should have killed him when I had the chance."

"It wasn't important," Jane apologized and backed quickly out the door.

Jane went to the restroom and splashed cold water on her face. "She should have killed him when she had the chance? What did that mean? I'm deceiving Pat. Is Pat deceiving the police, the IRS and me? Who are the bad guys, here?"

Pat came out of the office at closing time, looking drained and pale. A bit of her beauty had vanished, but her face still lit up when she said, "I need a drink. Do you want to come along?"

They took separate cars and a scary thought jumped Jane's brain. "Was there any reason for Pat to recognize this car? After all, it does belong to Alex." They parked next to each other in a crowded lot and when Jane got out, Pat was staring at the Subaru. "Is something wrong?" Jane whispered.

"I don't know." Pat looked confused. "I guess I was thinking of another time or place."

They settled in at the bar and Pat ordered a double Martini.

The drinks arrived and Pat slammed half of hers in one swallow, pulled out her cell phone and started punching buttons. "Honey, I've stopped for a drink. Don't wait up. Another day of dialing for dollars with the IRS. I'll see you in the morning. Love you, too." Her thumb severed the connection.

"My 'ex.' What a shitty excuse for a human being. He sent letters to the IRS for years and dragged my ass in and out of court for eight years of divorce proceedings. It's like 'Get over it," 'Move on,' 'Get a life,' all of those corny clichés that pertain to losers. His hatred for me was like a cancer. It wouldn't go away without treatment. He refused treatment and he died, but he's still reaching out from the grave to get even." Pat drained the rest of her drink and ordered a second.

Jane finished half of her Martini. She felt hot and flushed.

"Let's toast to assholes," she slurred. "Mine broke my heart when he filed for divorce. I believed he would stick by me. He spent half of the illegal money and never questioned where it came from. I mean, he knew what my salary was, but he took the vacations and drove the new cars for five years."

"Yeah," Pat added, "When they're spending, it's a different story. Paul would take $5,000 hunting trips, but when I charged cruise tickets for our daughter and myself, he tore up my credit cards. He went insane. Wait, he was already insane," Pat laughed. "He needed to be on medication, Prozac or something."

Jane was inebriated and almost said, "Yeah, that's what Alex told me." Like Pat wouldn't recognize the name of the woman that went to prison for her. Jane's liquid courage prompted a question. "Don't you just wish you could kill them all and get away with it?"

Pat turned toward Jane and said softly, "I thought about it, but I couldn't do it."

"I need a restroom," giggled Jane and pushed herself away from the bar with her legs spread. "Reminds me of getting off a horse." She grinned crookedly and staggered away.

When she returned Pat said, "It's obvious you're out of condition for drinking. Leave your car and I'll bring you back in the morning. I have every thing you'll need."

Jane only remembered the offer of a new toothbrush and then the alarm clock went off. She showered, dressed and carefully rolled up the long legs of her borrowed clothes before attempting the stairs. She followed voices until she found them in a sunlit breakfast area.

Pat's husband stood, offered his hand and smiled warmly, "I'm Walter and don't even think you can keep up with my wife when she decides to drink. She puts me to shame. Welcome."

Pat dropped Jane at her car and sat staring again. "Oh, please," Jane thought, "don't let her read the license plates. Why didn't Jake pre-think this slip-up?

18

_____

"Too long a sacrifice can make a stone of the heart"
William Butler Yeats, Easter In Michael Robartes and the Dancer

The JUDGE

The Judge pulled the offensive silk sheet to his neck. He could hear Clare's water in her bathroom and decided he had better let her know about Jenny's latest visit to his courtroom.

The slight crack in the bathroom door revealed a steamy view of Clare's enormous rear end. When they first married they were the same height and within twenty pounds of each other. Now her ass resembled an overstuffed chair. He had visions of slapping on some chintz fabric and offering her big butt to the public at a garage sale.

"Clare, can I talk to you?" he called, with a slight rap on the door.

"Oh Lord, you startled me. What are you doing, skulking around my room?" Her whiny, high-pitched voice grated on him like an inexperienced bow on an untuned violin.

"I need to talk to you about Jenny."

"Can't it wait until morning," she moaned. "I still have some invitations that need addressing."

"It can't wait. She was in my courtroom again this morning. This time there were vandalism charges. Her friends are dragging her around town with spray paint and I had to fine the whole group. As you know, the fines are coming out of our pocket."

"Well dear, we can afford it. Now I have to get these invitations out for our farewell party."

The Judge cocked his head and repeated, "Your farewell party?"

"Oh dear, don't act stupid. You know Jenny and I planned to leave for Europe next week. She does have to get away from those friends and everything will be normal when we return." Clare offered a small condescending smile and pushed past him toward her $12,000 antique desk.

Her left hip clipped his leg and caused him to rock, off balance. "Damn," he thought, "She can't even judge the enormity of her own body. Can money actually change a reflection in a mirror?" He stared sadly at the woman who was no longer aware of his pathetic existence.

On the way back to his room, he heard the same, high-pitched voice, "James, don't forget to pick up the dry cleaning and another case of that good wine on your way home tomorrow. The Bridge Club is playing here again."

Anger replaced his sadness. He was afraid Clare would end up killing Jenny out of sheer negligence. Her self-centered, altered personality was devoid of feelings for her own daughter.

He dropped his slippers and slid into the bed with the cold satin sheets Clare had selected. He had come to despise, damn near, every choice that Clare had inflicted upon him.

19

"I can be expected to look for truth, but not to find it."
Denis Diderot, Pensees Philosophiques

JANE

It was Tuesday morning and Jane answered the phone an hour before the club opened. She heard Pat's voice, "I figured I would find you there. I'm taking the entire day off. My daughter, Erica, is flying in. If anything urgent comes up you can reach me on my cell phone, but it had better be super-critical. Bye."

Jane's head turned toward the office door and she decided she was going in, if "turd-head" did not show up by her usual 9:00 a.m. It was 10:15 and Jane had gone through every file cabinet. There was no trace of any letters or threats from Paul. It was strictly health club books and records.

Jane took a lunch break and when she drove past their usual restaurant, she spotted Pat's Jaguar. No one was entering or exiting, so she quickly jumped out and peered through the Jag's windows. She almost slapped her forehead in a Three Stooge's gesture. "Of course," she said out-loud. "Her laptop. Who needs hard copy? She probably scanned everything in and now works in the privacy of her own little computer hell."

Jane finished her shift, coaxing obese people to their limits and then spent an extra hour on payroll. When she finally collapsed at her apartment door, it was midnight.

She noticed the faint odor of cologne. She left the lights off and crept through the kitchen. She peered around to the living room and saw the faint outline of Frankenstein on her balcony.

"Jake? Is that you?" When he turned, she blurted, "Jeeps, you scared the crap out of me. Don't you ever knock or use a phone?"

The sparkling white smile reflected the moonlight. "I like my women slightly aroused," he joked.

"Yeah, well, large doses of adrenaline are not exactly the bio-chemical ingredients for arousal." She was still shaking.

"Syd tells me, Pat might have recognized the car."

"Well, she sure stared at it long enough and she had this strange look on her face like a memory loss. Whatever, I panicked."

"It's all cleaned up," he assured her. "I called in a favor from Jimmy Hausmann, an old college buddy. There is now one dealership between Alex and your name on the title." He flashed his great smile again and asked, "What have you gotten so far?"

Jane could feel the depression written all over her face. "She must have everything on her laptop, because there's nothing at the health club."

"I'll check it out discreetly," he grinned again. "We got another client off today. By the time Alex is out, Vic will be all over the front pages."

"Don't you ever want to be that front-page attorney?" Jane asked.

"Naw, doing it this way is much more fun. I love winding up the rope that hangs them. If you can get away next weekend, I think you should see Alex. She's slipping. Her eyes never met mine once this morning."

"It's the one year blues," Jane informed him. "It's the realization that you're in for a long time. It slaps you in the face knowing it will be one year after another."

"I don't know what it's called, but she's not herself anymore, humor's gone and she's real distant. She didn't laugh once with Syd. We're both worried."

"I'll be there," Jane replied. Jake ruffled her hair and said, "Don't do anything else until you hear from me. I'll call you tomorrow night."

20

"The law hath not been dead, though it hath slept."
Shakespeare, Measure for Measure

JANE

Jake did better than call. Jane walked to her door and there was a post-it note. "Didn't knock or call, but I'm here." She stomped through the living room and ranted, "How the hell did you get in? I just had the locks changed."

"Stop wasting your money on locks. It's one of my special talents and I have to keep in practice." His flashy grin spit back the reflection of the overhead light.

"I picked up some Chinese and a bottle of wine." The boom box pumped slow, soft jazz notes through the room like tentacles. They drifted toward the patio door, as if trying to escape and Jake appeared to be blushing.

Jane felt uncomfortable and hurriedly began opening the little white containers. Jake turned to open the wine and once they sat down, Jane began twirling her chopsticks and pushing her food into small circles.

Without looking up, she said, "Something keeps bothering me, Jake. Alex has been in that depressing place for a year. What made you re-open the case now?"

"Poor Syd spent months running around to various law offices but no one was convinced that she had enough evidence to overturn the ruling. She found some 'hack' to file an appeal but it never got past Judge Manning. When she finally got around to us, we questioned the fact that Alex didn't get the death sentence. That sparked our curiosity. It seems Syd just kept repeating that Alex could never kill someone; it just wasn't in her nature. No real defense at all. We focused on the fact that she was only sentenced to fifty years with no parole."

"Considering that she's almost fifty, that is pretty much a life sentence," Jane said bitterly.

"Yeah, but, considering it was ruled murder, it's a light sentence. When we got hold of the court records, her confession was the sole basis for the conviction. The police never found any weapons and there was no disclosure of the autopsy reports. Alex broke down in court and never testified. The fact that Alex had a motive contributed to her guilt. She was never secretive about her arguments with Paul and several people knew about his gun games.

Jane remembered a conversation with Alex. Alex was pacing the cell, rubbing her hands up and down over her arms in a pathetic, self-embrace. She spoke rapidly, "A couple of loud noises woke me up. It was like the tail end of a fireworks display, only I couldn't see any lights. Then I heard the sound of an outboard motor and there was a slight reflection about fifty feet in front of the boathouse. I could see the vague outline of a boat, speeding away. I put the incident out of my mind until the next weekend, when the girls came to visit. We lifted the cover off the hot tub and it was empty. We walked around to the lakeside and saw five bullet holes in it."

Jake sat motionless for a few minutes, and added, "Vic thought it was worth examining the Coroner's report and I almost dropped my drawers when I read the part about four bullets in Paul's body. That gave pre-meditated murder a completely new meaning. How many killers stand in front of their victim, put three bullets into him, switch guns and shoot him again?"

"God," said Jane. "If a jury heard any of that information, Alex wouldn't have been convicted at all. There were too many discrepancies for them to be one hundred percent convinced of guilt."

"Like I said, Jane, it was pretty much a slam-dunk case and a lot easier than leaving another unsolved murder in the police files. A tax payer wouldn't want to pay for extensive, expensive detective work if there was a perfectly motivated suspect, with a signed confession, sitting in the court's lap."

Jane wondered how many of the women in prison had the same slam-dunk.

Jake sensed her thoughts, "Like you always say, some of them just slip through the cracks."

21

"I want to seize fate by the throat."
Ludwig Van Beethoven, letter to Dr. Franz Wegeler

ALEX

Alex returned to her cell and picked up her paper and pencil. She attempted to write down the daily, shitty occurrences, not that she would ever forget a minute without having to read it.

She was into the third paragraph when she felt the weight of another presence. She slowly turned and saw an enormous black figure leaning on her cell door. The outline stretched up about six feet, slim, but solid, with arms that made the seams on her orange shirt stretch to bursting at the biceps. Even the usual, baggy pants were tight across her thighs.

There was a huge mass of hair surrounding her head in an, almost, halo-like shape. When she moved into the full light of Alex's cell, the four-inch scar on the side of her face took on the shape of a big zipper. A yellow, waxy looking welt replaced what would have been a normal eyebrow.

"Close your mouth, Honky, you looks stupid.

Alex snapped her gaping mouth closed and blinked rapidly.

"Ah was Mindy's friend, the only one she talked to, 'sides the shrink."
She looked Alex up and down the way a predator examines its prey prior

to dining, head slightly bobbing and almost audibly sniffing. "She thought you mighta' been an angel. Dat girl was a mess." She chuckled in a low, raspy voice.

"Wwwwhat's your name?" Alex stammered.

"Yolanda," and she barked out a laugh. "Call me Yo, that's what Jane calls me."

"She thought you was smart. Now, she goes and axes me to keep my eye on you. I will, but you don't look like no angel to me."

Alex flashed on Sydney's and her own putrid little imitation of "Yo Ho" and there was a whole new meaning to "Yo" and the word fear.

"I can keep you safe in here, but I ain't sure I can get your humor back. Jane wants it all." Her huge shoulders shook and she barked out another chuckle.

Alex watched her dark shadow disappear around the corner of the cell and wondered if beatings and death had any comic value. What did Jane think that giant could do for her sense of humor?

22

"Skepticism is the first step toward truth."
Denis Diderot, Pensees Philosophiques

JANE

Jane was on the phone when the door swung open and Pat struggled through, carrying a large box, labeled Toshiba. She headed straight to the office, but couldn't get the door. Jane rushed to assist and Pat dumped the box on the desk, looking red-eyed and frazzled. "You will not believe what happened to me last night. My car window was shattered while Walt and I were in a restaurant. The thieves stole my laptop, car stereo, CD's, and kid gloves.

"Oh, no. Well, you can replace almost everything, except for all of the information in your laptop."

"Shit, it's all backed up on disks at home, but it's the inconvenience of downloading, the time, the energy. And, it's audit time; again, I just don't need this aggravation."

Jane began to feel slightly guilty and then reminded herself that this woman's ex-husband tortured Alex emotionally and now the truth finally had to come out. "Good-bye guilt, hello, new suspect," she thought.

"Can I help in anyway?" Jane offered.

"Just run this damn club, while I re-structure my internal stuff and I'll be grateful," Pat offered a miniscule smile.

Around 6:00, Pat emerged from her office and said, "I need a drink, Jane, want to join me?"

They took the recently vandalized Jaguar and Jane tried to offer comfort. "At least they didn't do the key scratching or tire slashing."

Pat turned toward her briefly and said, "I think it's about a lot more than robbery."

"What else could it be besides robbery?" Jane asked innocently and suddenly the name, Jake, clanged like a church bell in her head.

"Someone looking for much more than equipment." Pat's blond hair was caressing the side of her face and Jane couldn't clearly see her expression, but the solemn tone in her voice indicated a defeatist attitude that Jane wouldn't have associated with Pat.

23

"When I survey my past life, I discover nothing but a barren waste
of time, with disorders of the mind very near to madness."
Samuel Johnson, Prayers and Meditations

DAVID

They brought David to the local police station for questioning but his
mind was teetering on the edge of an abyss. His body kept rocking in an
imitation of his mind's precarious position.

They kept asking questions and he could not stop the faces and names
from blurring his vision. Was he speaking the names out-loud? Could they
read his mind? Paul started it all and I could have shot him if that traitor,
Sam, hadn't shown up. That jerk left me, just like Paul and Alex. They all
had to die. I had to protect myself.

David relived the excitement. How many ways can you kill an animal?
Poison, bow and arrow, shotgun, pistol, knife, or maybe, trapped. He had
done it all.

What were they asking him now? If he refused to talk, that would solve
everything. He thought if he stayed quiet, it would all go away. They just
couldn't know about all the others.

Alex took care of Paul. That was a surprise for that weak bitch, David
thought. She never should have left me, but then he remembered that

eventually she would have had to die. She wasn't stupid. She would have connected the disappearances of all the people he knew.

"They won't find them all, he thought, they're not all buried, some are in the pond, drowned, like rats." He almost smiled and caught himself, as his reflection bounced back from the one-way window. They are watching, he thought. I only have three or four to finish and then I can do honest work again and all of this will disappear.

I can't concentrate with all of these questions, he thought. My blood pressure is too high, I'm dizzy. Maybe I should just tell them everything and get the respect I deserve; after all, I eliminated most of the liars and cheaters.

24

"Man may his fate foresee, but not prevent
'Tis better to be fortunate than wise."
John Webster, The White Devil

The JUDGE

The Judge was reading the morning paper and he stared incredulously at the photo of David, on page two. "I remember this jerk," he thought out-loud. Some real estate swindle and David was called in, from up north. What an expert witness. David reviewed the appraisal on the property in question and found several faults in the report that would have diminished the appraised value. He was so cocky and self-assured, to the point of being obnoxious. The Judge continually reminded him to only answer the questions and stop rambling.

When the verdict was in, David was outside of the Judge's chambers and invited him to trap shoot on his property. David said anytime would be appropriate.

A month passed and one Saturday when Clare and Jenny were working their way toward their most extravagant shopping spree, the Judge was truly bored and decided to drive the two hours to David's forty acres.

The Judge was driving his new Mercedes, a twin to Clare's new vehicle. They delivered them a week ago, while he was sleeping. The delivery included the "pick-up" of his favorite, ten-year old, BMW. He had developed a bond with that car and was going to keep it forever, until Clare had other ideas.

The Judge hated the Mercedes and only agreed to drive it until he could get back his BMW, which Clare assured him, would never happen.

He arrived at David's around 12:30. There was no sign of life, until he heard a tractor or some small engine from behind the garage. He picked up his .410 and decided to look around. He walked up a recently trimmed path and guessed, again, at the engine sound. It was a front-end loader. He rounded a curve and saw two rectangular spaces about three feet by six feet in size. He saw new earth piled nearby and, for a moment, he had the cold, eerie feeling that he was in a cemetery. He was still feeling the anger over his new car, the loss of his BMW, and the "to-do" lists from Clare and, for a brief second, he visualized Clare lying in one of those worm-ridden spaces.

He heard a horn, retraced his steps on the path, and saw a truck pulling into the driveway. A wiry, middle-aged man jumped from the truck, plucked his weapon out of the back and offered his hand. Sam. He was there to shoot with David and the Judge offered an excuse involving wrong dates and times. They shook hands and the Judge got back into the big blue monstrosity, cursing his way back home, not knowing that he would never see that man alive again.

25

The JUDGE

The Judge reclined on the over-stuffed mattress of his king-sized bed, but sleep would not come. He dwelled on relationships. He didn't have the kind of friends you would call and say, "Guess what? I have cancer." The closest human being on earth was his daughter and she virtually hated him.

If he allowed Clare to parade Jenny around Europe, she would rebel. The girl needed to do things people her age were doing. If he went along and made the effort to direct her to interesting activities she could avoid most of Clare's weird acquaintances, but he would rather lose a testicle than spend two months with Clare.

Sleep was no longer an option so he went to his desk and began sorting through bills. The bar tab for the country club was $3,500 for one month. His eyes bugged when he found the $2,760 invoice from Vitellis Gourmet Shoppe.

Had Clare lost her mind? Europe would probably cost $20,000 for hotels, transportation and food alone. If the cow purchased gifts, art or clothes, that amount could double. He could no longer think clearly and his mind danced back to David's forty acres and the curious rectangular shapes. "Stop, stop," he ranted, rubbing his temples and then he heard the screeching of brakes outside.

He rushed to the window and watched a bright red Firebird skid to a halt. The doors swung open and three bodies fell out. The motor was revving loudly and a pounding base reverberated through the darkness. His daughter's underweight frame flew to the top of the pile and they all rolled around hooting and hollering to the beat of that horrendous bass.

The Judge was stunned into silence as he watched the bodies untangle with sloppy kissing and fondling. All but his daughter returned to the car and the Firebird screeched out of the concrete driveway leaving huge, black rubber tracks that swayed left and right, almost matching the exaggerated stagger of his only child.

In that moment, the Judge made his decision to change their future.

26

"I was much further out than you thought
and not waving but drowning."
Stevie Smith, Not Waving but Drowning

JANE

Jane slid her key in her lock and as she opened the door, she could recognize Jake's cologne mixed with an unidentifiable fishy odor. She peeked into the kitchen and gaped at the pots and pans strewn over the counters. Steam wafted from the stove in giant billows that tapered to comet tails circling the ceiling.

Jake stood like an immense statue with a blue and white apron tied tightly over his denim shirt and Dockers. His dark haired head turned to Jane and he teased, "Home from the wars, my little weight lifter?"

"Are there any pans or dishes you haven't used or should I run to the store and purchase more?" She joked.

"No, no, I've got this gourmet meal under control," but in the midst of his last word, a high-pitched squeal sounded and Jane's eyes focused on the tall, silver kettle on the stove.

"I don't think the Lobster twins are too pleased with their new environment." He glanced at the kettle.

"Lobster," Jane repeated. "Are we celebrating something tonight?"

"Nah, it's going to be more like comfort food. You're going to need a good meal and maybe a bottle of wine before I give you my latest news."

He would not discuss any of his recent findings until they were taking their last bites.

"And now, dessert," Jake smiled.

"Oh, please, Jake. The deprivation of information is killing me. What is happening?"

"We were granted a search warrant for David's house and we found the rifle that matched David's bullet, the bullet they removed from Paul's shoulder. David didn't kill Paul and now he's out on bail." Jake looked down at the table and examined a minimal scratch with forensic detail.

"Oh hell, then it has to be Pat." Jane rushed to a conclusion that did not involve Alex.

"Hold on, Jane. There was something extremely unusual with David's questioning and responses. Even though he knew he didn't kill Paul, he was unbelievably nervous. David admitted that he despised Paul, but he didn't think Alex would ever stand up to him, so he decided to put some fear in Paul's life by shooting a few holes in his house. He admits he was there that night. He was at the lakeside of the house and Paul was sitting at a table in front of the picture window. David took aim at something behind Paul's head and at the exact moment he squeezed the trigger, a car door slammed and Paul jumped up. The gun fired and he hit Paul's right shoulder."

"Then David is responsible for attempted murder. That clears Alex." Jane grinned.

"Not exactly. The other three bullets, that did kill Paul, didn't match any of David's guns. Those three bullets centered in Paul's chest.

"David said he ran to his car, which was parked next to Paul's snowplow and he saw Alex's car at the front of the driveway. More damn incriminating evidence against Alex."

"The only up side of this is that Paul probably lost so much blood from David's shot it could explain why he dropped to the floor. His angered expression means he must have believed Alex shot him from the front window before she even fired the shot at the doorway."

"You were right. I did need comfort food. I'll be up all night wondering what to do next." Jane groaned.

"Stay on the path you're on, Jane, unless you aren't comfortable anymore. If you're nervous or scared, get out." Jake offered. "You don't need to be doing this."

"Yes, I do. Maybe Alex shouldn't have stooped to Paul's level but she never intended to kill him and she shouldn't be spending the rest of her life in that 'pig pen' for him."

"I worry about you, Jane and I'm going to be sticking real close to you until this is over." Jake smiled and rubbed the back of his hand up and down the side of her face. She blushed, but she was also shocked at the electricity his touch provoked.

27

"All men that are ruined are ruined on the side of their
natural propensities."
Edmund Burke, Letters on a Regicide Peace

JANE

Jane was back at the health club working with a new, female member.
The girl was bench-pressing 125 pounds as if it were a yardstick. Jane was
watching with admiration when she felt a tap on her shoulder. She turned
to face Pat whose face was full color graffiti that spelled disappointment.

"Where did you get the car, Jane?" she questioned.

"Some dealership in Middleton," Jane answered. "Why?"

Pat's response was almost inaudible. "I vaguely remembered seeing
that car somewhere and when I checked the motor vehicle records, it was
tracked back to only two previous owners. One of them was Alexandra
Anderson. That name should ring a bell," she whispered.

Jane glanced over to a tall redhead standing near the door. "Hang on
and I'll explain, just let me help this customer."

"She's not a customer, Jane. She's your replacement. Goodbye." Her
face was devoid of all emotion. She turned and slowly walked toward her
office.

Jane was stunned and humiliated, as if Pat had slapped her. She went to the counter, picked up her purse and jacket, feeling light-headed and unbelievably guilty. She was a common criminal caught in the act of deception, with no alibi or excuse.

She barely had the strength to pull open the door and get into the car she predicted would be her downfall. She didn't remember the drive to her apartment but somehow her fingers automatically dialed Jake's number.

He was only halfway through the door when Jane repeated the conversation and his fabulous, white smile returned.

"You've done your job, Jane" he beamed. "We have copies of everything from her laptop, including incriminating letters that provide a real motive for killing Paul. One of the other great finds was in her glove compartment, a gun permit for a .22 caliber revolver. It has to be at her house. Now, you have further incriminating evidence.

Jane looked at him with a non-comprehending stare.

His smile widened, "She vaguely remembered seeing that car somewhere. That pretty much puts her at the scene of the crime, right?"

Jane impetuously grabbed Jake in a tight hug.

Jake held her at arms length, smiling. "I want you to come with me for a few hours, ok?"

"Well, it's not like I have a job anymore. I guess I could spare a couple of hours," she giggled.

"Bring a warm coat," he said.

28

"Character is always known. Thefts never enrich; alms never
impoverish; murder will speak out of stone walls."
Ralph Waldo Emerson, commencement address, Harvard Divinity School

JANE

They drove to Sam's house, about eight miles north of Medicine Lake.
Jane waited in the car for ten minutes and when Jake came striding out,
he blurted, "Something's not tracking here. Sam's wife said he left for a
ten-day hunting trip in Canada. That was twelve days ago and he hasn't
called. I think we need a quick stop at the local police shop."

They entered a small building and three feet in front of them was a
burly woman who could have been the poster child for marine recruits. She
loomed over a tiny table that had seen better days. One lonely officer sat
in a swivel chair behind her, his feet planted on the desk, across an open
newspaper. The only other item on the desk was a computer in the off mode.

"Who's in charge?" Jake boomed. His voice startled the officer, whose
legs flailed, knocking over the wastebasket. His angled eyeballs and curved
thumb directed their attention to a tiny office behind his desk.

Jake entered without knocking and an older, gray-haired man rose
slowly from his chair.

"To what do I owe this unexpected visit?" He asked.

"I need your help and some information ASAP," Jake barked. "Where could I find records of unsolved disappearances within the past fifteen years?"

"Depends on what you're looking for and who the hell you are." He challenged.

"Sorry," Jake stretched out his hand. "My name is Jake Hartnett and I work for an attorney, named Victor Morose. I have a very strong suspicion that you have a serial killer in your jurisdiction."

Jane's eyes exploded into enormous circles of disbelief. Had Jake gone mad?

The man behind the desk showed no expression. He held out his hand and grasped Jake's, "Benjamin Norris, Ben is good enough. He gave no smile or evidence of suspicious doubt.

Ben continued, "You looking for kids, little girls or women?"

"All disappearances," Jake answered, emphasizing the word all.

"Go back out the door, shoo that worthless idiot, Stuart from his desk and type Missing in his computer. Stuart has an IQ somewhere south of room temperature. Follow the prompts on the screen and have at it. And on your next visit, knock."

"Thank you, sir."

Jake politely moved Stuart aside and seven folders below Missing, he started pulling up names. He went back fifteen years and found fourteen names, astonishing for such an unpopulated area. Jake printed out the information and they hurried to their car.

"I need to get this information to my buddy at the Bureau and then we're going out for a premature celebration dinner." Jake exuded enthusiasm.

"What makes you so sure your theory is correct?" Jane asked.

"It's what I'm good at. I seem to have intuition when it comes to suspects," Jake replied. "David was off the walls in the interrogation room and when Alex said he used to bang his boots and telephone on his desk, I questioned the amount of control he had over his temper. I think he's very capable of losing it."

Jane looked at the satisfied grin on his handsome face and realized there was something extremely seductive about a person who has found their niche in life and therefore, enjoyed life in general as opposed to the poor majority that drag their butts to the same boring or stressful job everyday. She returned his smile.

29

"The older I grow, the more I distrust the familiar doctrine
that age brings wisdom."
H. L. Mencken, Prejudices: Third Series

JANE

Jake was on the phone with Sam's wife. She watched his expression fill with sympathy as he hung up the phone.

"She's crying. She hasn't heard from anyone since she filed the Missing Persons Report. She called Sam's hunting guide in Canada and he confirmed that Sam never showed up. "Something is sucking like a vacuum. I have a bad feeling that Sam won't be coming home."

Jane flashed back to a conversation she had with Alex and her mouth opened with an audible, sharp intake of air.

"Jake, Alex told me about a day she and Paul spent at David's. He has forty acres of land that he's turned into a shooting range with traps and targets all over the place."

"Say no more. I'll swing by David's and meet you back at the hotel later," he suggested.

"Not a chance, detective," she admonished. "I spent fifteen years as a boring CPA and I believe I'm finally entitled to a serious, action-packed adventure on the front lines."

"One quick stop at the hardware store before dinner and then your adventure will terminate with you waiting in the car while I do a little investigating," he smiled.

They sat in a small booth with a red and white, checked tablecloth and a wine bottle candle that cast flattering, dancing shadows across their faces. Jane was becoming anxious thinking of her upcoming journey to the unknown.

As if sensing her thoughts, Jake reached over and took her hand. "Remember, you're only coming along to remain in the car. You'll call Chief Norris if I'm not back in thirty minutes."

The frail, mustached owner stopped at their table, glanced at their intertwined hands and smiled. "We hava speciala cake for the newlyweds," and his gold rimmed, front tooth sparkled in the candle light.

They politely declined and Jane said, "Pretty sad statement for lengthy relationships, I mean, you don't hold hands unless you're newlyweds."

"I wouldn't let that happen," said Jake. "Have you ever read William Butler Yeats?"

"Try me." Jane smiled.

> "When you are old and gray and full of sleep
> And nodding by the fire, take down this book,
> and slowly read.
> How many loved your moments of glad grace,
> And loved your beauty with love false or true,
> But one man loved the pilgrim soul in you,
> And loved the sorrows of your changing face."

This time there was no blush or embarrassment and Jake looked into Jane's eyes

"This man cannot possibly be for real," Jane thought.

They were holding hands and leaning on each other as they left the restaurant. As Jake opened her car door, she was beginning to feel some anxiety; her big adventure was hanging like a dark, rain-filled cloud in the immediate future of this starless night.

30

"Fear is the main source of superstition, and one of the main sources of cruelty. To conquer fear is the beginning of wisdom."
Bertrand Russell, An Outline of Intellectual Rubbish

JANE

Jake slowed the Jeep to a stop about a quarter mile from where David's forty acres started.

"Ok, lock the doors after I get my stuff from the back. Keep the cell phone on your lap. Stay low and don't unlock the doors until you see my face."

His lips brushed her cheek and Jane wished she could feel them on her lips for the first and maybe the last time. She wasn't feeling quite as adventurous as she felt in the safety of her apartment. She wondered how many times Jake had done this before and if he really enjoyed this part of his job.

Her chest felt tight and she knew she wasn't breathing regularly; it was too rapid and shallow. She heard the back door softly close and she wondered if she would be feeling this frightened if she didn't care for him. Yes, was her immediate response. She was a boring, sheltered accountant.

The silence increased her panic more than her negative thoughts. She heard a twig break and told herself it was just a raccoon or some stupid, woodsy creature.

She crawled toward the floor and checked her watch. Nine-thirty. She stayed low and waited for what seemed like an hour and then leaned toward the floor to check her watch. Nine-thirty-four.

The heavy silence was building. Each moment became a new brick laid in a wall. Soon, it would be a container for her fear. The sudden realization that she was trapped inside that wall came to her as another twig broke and panic flooded her shelter. She bent toward the floorboards but began to feel like her back was the perfect target for a bullet. She flashed on the light when she realized she couldn't remain there. She would rather die out in the open than in the car, like a guppy in a goldfish bowl. She crawled over the front seat and peered to the back. There was a shovel and a larger flashlight.

She opened the rear door, grabbed the equipment and slowly lowered the door until the light went out. She moved toward the ditch and followed it along the edge of what she prayed was David's property.

She felt her way along the trees and finally found a clearing. There was a path about three feet wide and she knew it would not have been there naturally. She was painfully aware that she wasn't an outdoorsy person and the strange sounds and darkness made her move like a turtle dragging a boulder. She heard more snapping branches, a dull thud, and then a low groan, followed by a high-pitched voice.

"You son of a bitch, I had everything under control until you came snooping around. I don't give a shit about Paul, but I did feel sorry for Alex, or maybe she deserved him. She left me, you know. She was smart and we could have built a great business together, but then Paul came along. Alex had brains but her taste in men sucked. She believed everyone that was kind to her, even if they were liars."

"Now, you have to join the others. I don't hate you; not like the others. You're just too close to finding the truth and I can't let that happen."

David raised his shotgun and took aim at Jake's head in the same instant that Jane swung the shovel. David's body collapsed on Jake who was lying in a shallow grave meant for someone else.

She struggled to get David's body off Jake, holding her breath to avoid the putrid stench surrounding them. As she tried to revive Jake to full consciousness, she leaned on bones still attached to flesh. It had to be Sam. Her stomach tightened into a convulsive spasm and she scrambled to the top of the grave to regurgitate several times before Jake regained consciousness.

31

"If you walked into a room and saw everyone's troubles
hanging on a wall, you'd head straight to your own."
Anonymous (Jewish Saying)

JANE

Jane was sitting on the couch, closest to the phone. She had not moved since reading Jake's note.

"I had to run out this evening. I'll be back with snacks and wine. If you're too tired, just go to bed and I'll wish you pleasant dreams. P.S. Lock the door, I don't need a key."

Jane venomously blurted, "You could have taken me along, you big jerk, after all, I saved your butt last time."

She looked anxiously around the small living room trying to focus on anything to take her mind off Jake. She didn't buy a TV, never thinking this mission for Alex would take this long. In the beginning, she had the ten, twelve-hour workdays; suddenly, her entire focus was on Jake. Now that she knew the risks he took for his job, she either had to be a part of it or get off the bus and catch a different ride toward her unplanned future.

Jane was still pacing in circles when the door opened. Jake smiled and tossed a pizza on the counter.

"You humungous jerk," she cried. "How could you leave me here to worry? I need to do these things with you."

Jake moved toward her, picked her up and finally kissed her. A great, long, drawn-out kiss, with just the right amount of hard and soft combined. Jane could feel her pulse speed up. She inhaled his cologne and felt the hardness of his body. She never wanted that kiss to end. When he finally set her back down, they hugged tightly. They swayed and stayed that way for many comforting moments.

When the feeling of comfort mutated to a new, highly erotic sensation, they forgot about the pizza. Jake, once again, swept her in his arms and Jane began discarding clothes along the hallway.

She watched as he slowly removed his clothes and when he gently lowered himself to the bed, he brushed her hair from her face and kissed every place her curls had vacated.

It felt as though hours passed while they explored each other's bodies and a variety of positions. Each new, audible gasp, breath or moan was an education on what each enjoyed, needed, wanted or desired.

When they were near exhaustion, they flopped to their backs and their heads turned to exchange smiles across the pillow's edge.

"You seem to be the exact item that was missing in my life," Jake beamed.

Jane leaned up on one elbow and brushed his hair with the back of her hand. "I think what's missing in mine is the information you got at Pat's house," she smiled.

"Why you little half-pint, imitation detective. How did you know where I was?" he laughed and wrapped the blanket over her head.

When the giggling subsided, Jake explained that he picked up a search warrant from Judge Manning and then drove to Pat's house. He promised to tell her the details in the morning. They leaned into each other and entangled their bodies until their temperatures and breathing equalized. They drifted into a perfect sleep.

Jane awoke to the sound of pots and pans clanking in the kitchen. She threw on her robe and peered around the corner. Jake was wearing the blue apron, the table was set and fresh coffee was brewing. He offered her a glass of orange juice and a warm smile.

"I can see you're quite at home in this room," she teased.

"I'd better be. I'm a big boy, you know, and someone has to keep this furnace stoked."

"I think it would be cheaper to just hook you up to natural gas, but, tell me what's on our agenda today." Jane fished for the information they never got to last night.

"My quick search of Pat's house revealed some rather rewarding information. I found letters and cards from her daughter in her bedside drawer. They seemed to have a special relationship, more like sisters. The letter that caught my eye was dated the day of Paul's death and it was a culmination of a series of threats and lawsuits. Paul included a copy of a letter addressed to the District Attorney. Pat bought Erica a new car and took the title in the health club's name. Paul accused her of tax evasion, insurance fraud and misuse of corporate funds. Paul said he would make sure Pat would be prosecuted for every single break in the law."

"I also found her .22 caliber revolver. We'll get those results back within twenty-four hours. I have photos of the letters and Vic and I are going to set up a meeting with her this evening. I think she'll talk to us this time."

"I'll stop by later tonight with the details, if you promise to stay here, out of harm's way," Jake offered a lop-sided grin.

"I'll try, but remember, I'm used to having a cell mate." Jane grumbled.

"Would you settle for a cat or a parrot?"

32

"The wicked flee when no man pursueth."
Bible, Proverbs 28:1

PAT

Vic and Jake pulled to a stop in front of Pat's house. Jake glanced at his watch and said, "Let's go."

When the door opened, Walter appeared agitated and confused. His up-handed gesture to the opposite wall was all that was necessary to locate Pat.

She leaned on the kitchen table with her face buried in the crook of her elbow. She looked up with red-rimmed, watery eyes and gave a thin smile.

"Jane knew, didn't she?"

"Not really," Jake said. He added gently, "She was hoping she was wrong."

"I really like her. I kept hoping everything would just go away, but instead, it grew, surrounded by more and more suspicion and guilt." She looked at the floor.

"You can't let another human being pay for your actions." Jake warned.

"It was easier when I never knew anything about Alex. I could make things up in my mind to justify her sacrifice, but when I met Jane and figured out they were good friends, well, it just got more difficult. If you're the kind of person to have a friend who would do everything Jane did . . . ." Her face dropped to her hands again.

"Tell us what happened, Pat. I mean everyone knows Paul was a vindictive bastard. Maybe we can make sense out of this and even help you out." Jake offered.

"You can't help me," she whimpered. "I killed him."

Walter gasped. "What are you saying, Pat? You were here, with me, that night."

Pat looked up slowly with adoring eyes. "You can't help me this time, my love. I did shoot Paul." She looked at Jake. "I'll meet you at the police station tomorrow and sign a confession. Please tell Jane I am very sorry. She can have her job back, if there is any corporation left. Heck, she could run it while I'm in prison."

Walter kneeled at her side and gushed, "Oh God, please don't do this Pat. I need you, I love you, please."

Pat stroked his hair, the side of his face and softly kissed his cheek. "I'm sorry if I've disappointed you, Walt. I truly love you."

Vic and Jake let themselves out and once in the car, they sat in silence.

"Ok," Jake finally murmured. "For once, I don't crave the job. I see what Jane liked about Pat and if anyone deserved to be shot, it was Paul."

Vic started the car and as they inched away from the curb, he whispered, "Something still isn't right with all of this. Can you feel it?"

Jake nodded. "Yeah, I feel it, but where the heck is my intuition?"

33

"Violence is good for those who have nothing to lose."
Jean Paul Sartre, The Devil and the Good Lord

JANE

Jane and Jake were watching the ten o'clock news on an old television they borrowed from Vic.

"Bulletin . . . . Our 'on location reporter' is with us for the latest news break on the multiple bodies found on David Barkley's forty acre parcel. Four bodies were discovered in shallow graves and two more dredged from a pond. Reports indicate there will be more. Barkley is being held, with no bail, in a county facility. Local police are crediting the Sullivan Law Firm with the information that led to Barkley's arrest.

Jake snapped off the TV. "You know Jane, you used to try to convince me that Pat was a good person and I felt that same thing today. If it hadn't been for Alex, you two probably would have been great friends."

"Well, my friend and roommate, for almost a year, will be spending a portion of her life in less than pleasurable surroundings. I can't make new friends if they're keeping my old ones in harm's way."

"Jane, think of something that would make Pat do this. I can't figure out a logical explanation for a highly educated, intelligent person to risk everything to bump off an ex-husband. She's happily remarried and loves her daughter, her business is successful and Paul was, pretty much, out of her life for eight years, with the exception of threatening letters."

Jane shrugged and said, "Maybe it was a culmination of all of Paul's harassments, until she lost it. Anyway, think of Alex. She was highly educated, had a good business going and yet, she took a shot at Paul."

Jake looked slow and long at Jane and said, "This is what I'm talking about. I do not want to end up with another innocent victim sitting in prison. Something reeks. The whole case is starting to stink and the stench is stifling my intuition."

"Don't make me pick between them. I don't want either of them to be in prison. I don't know what's going on, but Pat is willing to sign a confession and Alex will get out. Heck, at least Pat could spend the same amount of time in prison as Alex did. It might be a rather humbling experience. Ask me."

He was quiet for a while and then, "I guess I will ask you, Jane. Why did you take the money?"

At first, Jane was stunned into silence and then reconciled herself to the fact that if anyone deserved an explanation, it was Jake.

"The insurance agent I worked for was cheating on his taxes and I was his accountant. He didn't care if I ended up in prison for his dishonesty. But, that really wasn't my only motivation. I hated what he was doing to his clients. He would quote policies to middle class families with $500,000 coverage and a $2,500 deductible. I started looking through files and discovered that he would write the policies for $300,000 with a $5,000 deductible. The few people that actually read their policies would call and he'd say it was a typo, not to worry. One or two people out of every twenty would catch it.

The final straw was the fine print clauses he would add to the written policy, such as, no teenagers could drive the vehicle. There was no coverage if any of their children had an accident. I, ignorantly, thought that if I didn't turn him into the IRS, I would end up in jail anyway, so it might as well be profitable. I think I've paid for my ignorance with five years out of my life.

Jake reached out and pulled her to him. "You have, 'Mighty Mouse,' and then some. You saved my life."

Jane moved closer, but then, ran her finger around the stitches in Jake's head where David had slammed the stock of his shotgun.

"Does that still hurt?" She asked.

"They shot me so full of Novocain at the hospital, I don't think I'll feel it for a week," he laughed.

Suddenly, the phone rang and Jane handed it to Jake. His face lost its grin and he hung up. "They just got the results on Pat's .22. Not only is it new, but it's never been fired."

34

"When you have eliminated the impossible, whatever remains,
however improbable, must be the truth."
A.Conan Doyle, The sign of Four, A Demonstration

PAT

Jane was watching Jake, Victor and Pat through a one-way window at the Medicine Lake Sheriff's office.

Pat was wearing a simple T-shirt and Levis, running shoes and a baseball cap and she still looked elegant. Her hair, styled in a half-hazard rendition of a ponytail, had streaked blond strands escaping all around the cap. Her eyes were red-rimmed and swollen. The dark circles below them were a depressing reminder of the fact that she had not slept all night.

"Gee," thought Jane, "pretty much the way it was for Alex, only about eleven months longer than Pat's one-night stand." Still, sympathy rose in her chest as she heard Pat's weak voice admit to being at Paul's house and seeing Alex's car parked right where it had been in crazy David's description.

Jane glanced behind her and recognized Chief Norris and his incompetent sidekick, Stuart.

She turned back to the window and when she saw and felt Pat's "melt-down," she took the time to question Ben.

"Do you think she shot Paul?"

"Strange, but I'm sort of hoping she didn't." That was the first sign of emotion Jane had ever associated with the Chief.

Pat was looking up again and said, "Let's get this over. Where should I start?"

Jane's attention was riveted to Pat's face, which, despite the lack of sleep was still engaging. Jane knew Jake's huge heart would find a way to make the present situation less painful for her.

"Pat, we know Paul was setting you up for a big fall concerning your daughter and the vehicle situation." Jake didn't finish.

Pat interjected with a questioning, slanted smile, "His last letter said he wouldn't rest until I was behind bars for anything he could think of. He would make my life miserable until I no longer had any contact with our daughter. He was going to take her away from me and I went crazy. I told Walter I had to leave in the morning to check on the only club I have in Missouri. I'd spend the night, check the books and be home the following day."

Was Walter the only one who knew you were supposedly going to Missouri?" Jake perched one leg on the seat of a chair and stared at her intently.

Pat's face turned a light shade of pink and she looked up. "Yes," she said firmly.

Chief Norris shot Jane a cynical look and said, "Bull."

35

"Victory awaits him who has everything in order_luck people
call it. Defeat is certain for him who has neglected to take the
necessary precautions in time_this is called bad luck."
Ronald Amundsen, cited in Diana Preston, A First Rate Tragedy

The JUDGE

"Bull," raged the Judge. He had Jenny grasped at the shoulders.

He decided to get out of the house for a while after the disturbing
display of drunken teens squealing around his driveway. As he made his
way through the four-car garage, he heard a soft moaning blended with a
few off-key notes from an unrecognizable song.

He walked around the Jeep and didn't see anything. He looked into the
boat and again, nothing. When he circled the Mercedes, the song, which
was half a moan, grew louder. At the far end of the garage, he saw Jenny
draped over the seats in the golf cart.

Her eyes were large, red streaked and rolling. Her soft soprano voice was
gasping the words to a hymn he remembered from his own childhood.

"Jesus loves me," shallow breaths, "this I know." An almost imperceptible
giggle followed, then, "we are weak," with more intermingled giggling."
"He is strong." Her voice gurgled to a choking rasp and a coughing spasm

wracked her chest. Her interrupted breathing faltered and then her eyes focused vacantly on the garage ceiling.

"Bull," the Judge barked again, "You're not leaving me this way." He let go of her shoulders and lifted her from the cart to the Mercedes. While he backed out of the driveway, he dialed the hospital. "I'm on my way, fifteen minutes or less. I suspect a drug overdose. Please be ready."

The stretcher waited in the circular drive and the attendants carried his only child to the entrance. His heart struck a panic peak as Jenny's body started jumping in bizarre, seizure type movements. He had to race to keep up with the stretcher. He was out of breath, hot and nauseous.

He thought of the driving rain that pounded the windshield all the way to the hospital. It was as if something evil was blowing against him.

His weakened breath shushed a meek, "Please God, don't let her die. I love this girl. I know I've been a poor example of how to live, but I love her."

Thunder rumbled and lightning struck nearby. "Please, God, I'll change, I'll care more and try harder. I'll do anything to help my daughter. Please, give me a second chance."

More lightning flashed and thunder grumbled like an old man clearing his throat. The lights flickered several times and the Judge was filled with an uneasy guilt that reminded him he might not be worthy of a response to his prayers.

He awoke several hours later in an uncomfortable, vinyl chair, three-feet from Jenny's bed.

When the Doctor entered, the Judge had a very bad feeling. He knew Jenny had not responded to any treatment last night, but he was unprepared for the actual diagnosis.

"I'm afraid there isn't any good news," he began and paused, "She's had a major drug overdose and may not regain consciousness. You may as well go home and try to get some sleep. There won't be any kind of change for several hours. By the way, someone called the hospital before you arrived and asked how Jenny was doing."

36

"Pray, for all men need the aid of the gods."
HOMER, Odyssey

The JUDGE

The Judge slowly opened the door to the immense entry and moved toward voices in the dining room, where another eleven strangers gathered. He scanned each face as the conversation died. The Judge stared back at them wondering, "Who are these people and where does my wife keep finding them?"

"Could you please excuse us for a moment?" He directed his attention to Clare. "I need to talk to you privately, Clare."

"Oh darling, can't it wait? We're only on our third course."

"It can't wait, damn it." The earlier moment's brief silence now stretched itself across the room like a two-ton spider web and for a second, the Judge felt like a fly.

Clare awkwardly slid her chair back, excused herself and waddled toward the living room. She opened and closed the ten foot, double doors and turned sharply toward the Judge.

"James, you are becoming an incredible bore and I will no longer tolerate your offensive behavior to my very important friends. I'm tired of your lack of interest in our dinner parties and . . . ."

Her mouth was still moving as the Judge grasped her wrist. "Stop talking and listen," he cautioned. "Jenny is in the Intensive Care Unit at the hospital. She's had a major drug overdose and is unconscious."

"Oh dear, this couldn't have happened at a worse time," she wailed. "We have a bridge game tomorrow, the fashion show Thursday, and we're leaving for Europe on Friday. She had better be well by then."

"Clare, the doctor said she may not regain consciousness."

"Oh, don't be ridiculous, James. We can't change the tickets to Paris. I'll just pick her up and she can recuperate in France. I have to go back into dinner now, they're all waiting. We can talk about this in the morning."

He watched her rainbow caftan sway toward the doors and there wasn't a logical response in his head. How do you argue with a rock? Reaching out to her made him feel like an ant at the end of a five hundred foot rope, swinging past an elephant, on a lift and rescue mission.

He stood gaping at the door and a single tear burned his cheek. He really had no one to talk to. What kind of an existence had he chosen?

He wandered to the kitchen and startled the cook into a hop and gasp.

"Oh Lord, Judge, you scared me. No one comes in here except you in the morning or Miss Jenny, late at night," she smiled mischievously. "I can always tell when she's been out late. There are chips and crackers all over the counters. She stops in during the day and apologizes, but I just say, it's ok, Miss Jenny, that's what I'm here for. She's a sweet girl, Judge."

"She actually talks to you, Margaret?"

"Almost everyday. I know who she's dating and who she's mad at." Margaret flashed a prim little smile at him.

"She's in the hospital. Seems she took some drugs. Too many." His voice broke and the tears started again. "I'm sorry," his voice trailed to a frail effusion of breath.

"Oh Lord, come here. It'll be alright." She reached for him, arms outstretched and he slowly moved toward the fold of her arms. They hugged and both wept.

"You get some sleep tonight and we'll both go see her in the morning." Her soft voice and the human touch brought him an unfamiliar sense of security and warmth.

He clung for a moment longer and moaned, "I can't make it without her, Margaret. I'd do anything to make it right."

"And you will. I knew that about you when I started here ten years ago. You're a good man, Judge and we'll save my little girl tomorrow. There isn't anything a good prayer can't handle."

37

"Caged birds accept each other but flight is what they long for."
Tennessee Williams, Camino Real

ALEX

Jane was sitting in the Visitor Center, on the right side for a change, and finally, Alex came through the door. She had lost, at least, another ten pounds. The orange creases of her uniform enveloped her shrunken frame and her skin blended into the pale beige walls. One of the creatures from "The Night of the Living Dead" shuffled toward Jane.

"Holy Crap, Jake wasn't exaggerating. You look like shit."

"Nice to see you, too, Jane."

"Jeeze, Alex, there's only two ingredients in your makeup, depression and defeat. What's up?"

"Just this place." Alex peered up from beneath a crooked slant of dark, brown hair that needed cutting, shaping and washing.

"Oh, like you didn't know it sucked the first day you arrived," Jane blurted.

"The loss of freedom and the loss of luxuries are nothing compared to the abused state of the women in here. They've never had a chance. They've been abused, lied to, and generally screwed over. Literally."

Alex, none of that is your fault and you can't change the world. Couldn't you see that from the outside?"

"I guess I was never exposed to that element in our society. Now, I'm one of them."

"You're not one of them, Alex, because you're a fighter. You'll fight back." Jane's voice was rising unsteadily.

"Jane, they gave the 'Mouse' kitchen duty. She didn't speak a word for a month and they thought it was safe to send her in among sharp utensils. She sliced her windpipe and jugular. What kind of life would bring someone to slice their own throat?" Alex was sucking in huge gasps of air and tears were flowing.

Jane sat quietly, waiting for the tear's to stop, not knowing what to say. She watched as the guard, Bertha, rose slowly and put a hand on Alex's shoulder.

"She wasn't going to get better, Alex. Shirley was gang raped years ago and has been in and out of institutions throughout the state. She wandered out of the last facility and robbed a convenience store. She ended up in here before the paperwork caught up with her. I'm just sorry she ended up in your cell."

"That's comforting, Bertha," Alex offered a lop-sided grin. "I can't wait to meet my next psychotic roommate."

Jane and Bertha exchanged glances and then Bertha winked.

38

"A man must find his occasions in himself, it is true."
Henry David Thoreau, Walden

JANE

Jane and Jake were driving along the Interstate, heading north. The overcast sky, filled with threatening, rain-laden clouds, darkened. Light drops sprinkled the windshield and Jane's thoughts tangled within her ears. She was straining to hear the splash that would connect her brain to one of sounds that was missing in prison.

When she and Alex shared their inner block, windowless cell there were no sounds of rain, wind or birds. No shrieks, no caws, no wings in flight. You couldn't even hear thunder. The sounds she fought to close out were the depressing sounds of fellow inmates. Cries in the night, snoring, praying, moaning and worst of all, crying. Soft, stifled sniffles, sobs, wailing and weeping that dragged through the dark hours.

Everything relating to nature was non-existent. The human element controlled everything, especially your heart.

"Jane?" Jake was stealing sidelong glances at her. "Are you OK?"

"Yes, yeah, I was just waiting to hear the sound of rain splashing somewhere. I really missed that sound."

Jake slowed and pulled the car to the side of the road. There was a deep gully and a small bridge that crossed a creek along the side of the highway. He jumped out and grabbed jackets from the backseat. He strode around the rear of the car and opened Jane's door.

"C'mon," he enticed. "I've got a good feeling that you'll get your wish in the next ten minutes."

They slid down the bank and walked toward the bridge as larger drops began filling the sky. They had barely picked their way around the end of the bridge when thunder clapped and a downpour gushed.

Jake laid an extra coat on the ground below the bridge and they sat. "Can't even think of not granting you your wish," he smiled. "It's too easy."

He wrapped his arm around her, her head leaned on his shoulder and they listened to the amplified droplets striking concrete. The rain ricocheted off the creek water, off the bridge and off the leaves of the trees. They sat in silence. Time stopped.

Jane savored every drip and drop and finally realized drops were running down her cheeks. It was dry under the bridge, but Jake's offering of fifteen minutes from his life meant more to her than regaining the sounds she had missed for five years. She turned her face up towards his and smiled the smile of a six year old on Christmas morning.

They were back on the road within thirty minutes and headed north to Paul's house.

"What exactly are we looking for?" Jane questioned.

"Anything the police and our own team might have missed. There must be a clue leading to Alex's gun."

They turned off the highway and headed down a long, winding road toward Buckskin Lake. Twelve miles later, they turned down a gravel road that wound through the trees along a river. Jane knew, from Alex's description, they were close. The sun was getting low in the sky and Jane had the smallest twinge of regret over their bridge detour. Since that night on David's acreage, darkness threatened her confidence.

The driveway had almost overgrown in the past year and Jake got out of the jeep twice to haul fallen trees to the side of the drive. They parked the car and Jake sat still, studying every direction from the car.

It was as though he had a tape recorder of every conversation with Alex in his head.

"Off to our right," he narrated, "you'll see parking spaces for two cars, David's and the snowplow. Just the way Alex said. Straight ahead is the entrance to Paul's and the doorway where Alex, allegedly shot Paul. There was no gun between her car and the house. There was no gun within fifty yards in any direction. Alex couldn't have thrown a gun fifty yards anyway."

Jake got out of the car and walked slowly toward the house. Jane followed, watching and studying every detail of her surroundings.

When they reached the door, Jake fumbled with the two copies of the keys from the initial investigation. He turned on the over-sized flashlight and examined every inch of the entrance.

Once they entered the hallway, he turned and looked back toward the door. "Alex was standing outside this door. She said she aimed high and to his right."

"Don't you think the police have gone over every detail of this place?" Jane asked.

"The investigation was handled by the local police and Alex was already assumed guilty from her own feeble confession of taking a shot at him." Jake grinned.

"Smells like there may be more bodies in here," Jane giggled.

"Well, it's been closed up for a year," but as he spoke, he took in smaller breaths. The fetid, musty odor that assailed his sense of smell was strong enough to affect his sense of taste. He turned to stare at a point on the opposite end of the room. The flashlight lit a twelve-inch, dark brown spot at the corner of the wall and ceiling.

Jane followed the light's beam and blurted, "Oh shit, he had the same thing Alex had at her house."

"What?" Jake waited.

"It's water damage from ice freezing under the shingles. Alex called it "ice damming" and it was common this far north."

Jake ventured forward and pulled a small knife from his pocket. They advanced on the dirty brown paneling and soggy drywall. Jake pulled on a surgical glove and poked gently. The saturated drywall crumbled like a milk-soaked cookie. He put the knife back in his pocket. "Won't need this," he mumbled. One more touch and a two-inch circle opened and the mushy drywall twisted and hung toward the floor.

"Wholly shit," he whispered.

"What? Jane prodded.

"We've got to call Victor. I think we just found Alex's bullet. We're going to need an infrared trajectory study on the bullet that's imbedded in the insulation. We can't let the local police in on our finding until the experts are all lined up. "This has to be precise." He began punching numbers on his cell phone and then rolled his eyes.

"I forgot we were up north. We have to get to a hotel and good old-fashioned land-lines. We've got a lot to do."

39

"Good families are generally worse than any others."
Anthony Hope, The Prisoner of Zenda

ALEX

The cell door opened and Bertha smiled while Yolanda walked through.

"Meet your new cellmate, Alex."

"Oh Bertha," grinned Alex. "I don't know how you pulled this off, but I'll be eternally grateful."

"Ain't sure how I feel about it. You are one crazy cracker, Alex." Yolanda actually smiled.

"Hell," Alex beamed. "It's been lonely in here and I'm sure Yo won't be slicing her throat or any vital organs."

"Ain't got no vital organs, no musical background at all." She grinned, setting the zipper into motion.

"Well, I'll leave you and your new roommate to get acquainted. I need a lunch break." Bertha swung her watermelons toward the door and cast one last wide grin in their direction.

"First off, ah don't take no bunks in the sky. You'll be sleeping up there."

"No problem. Got anymore complaints?"

"Heard from Jane?" Yo asked.

"Yesterday. The police and the Medical Examiner found all kinds of bodies on David's property. Jake said the place looks like an archeological dig. I think he planned to kill Paul and me when we were shooting there. Thank God, Sam showed up. Well, not so lucky for Sam, it seems. I still can't believe David was capable of multiple murders, I mean his temper would flare up at the drop of a hat, but if I were a betting person, I'd bet I was more capable of murder. I held everything inside and it seems that if you take more and more crap, your brain would eventually explode."

"Yeah, well, David filled up faster than you did. You ain't the world's genius on readin' people, Alex. Ain't nobody sure of what they'll do until they reach the edge." Yo's face gravitated toward the floor and Alex knew Yo's mind had wandered into a cold place. Alex thought about a hug, the way she and Jane comforted each other, but that definitely wasn't Yo's style.

"Hey, how's your mom and the kids?" Alex tried to keep her voice light, filled with fun.

"Don't go there, girl. My mom is old and strugglin'." She stretched out on her bunk with her face to the wall and the cell filled with a weighty, humid silence.

Take the chance, Alex thought. Spit it out and take a beating. This could be worth a concussion and a few broken ribs. She thought of how lucky she had been in prison, up to this point. Maybe it was time for a good ass whipping.

"Jane says she thinks Jake may be able to get you out of here. It might just take a little white lie." Alex realized her voice sounded weak and wimpy, even to her own ears.

Yo turned over and asked, "What you talkin' 'bout, Alex?"

"Jake talked to the doctor and three nurses who were in the Emergency Room the night they brought you in. They were frantic over how close you were to death. None of them could believe you didn't press charges against your husband.

Yo's mouth opened and stretched the zipper into a four-inch ruler.

"Wait, let me finish," Alex begged. "Jake says all it would take to get an appeal is for one witness to say your husband beat you, again, the night you came home from the hospital. Then it would be self-defense. I mean, look at what he already did to you. You were fresh out of the hospital, with hundreds of stitches."

"Dat ain't true, Alex. He didn't beat me and I ain't got no witness." Yo turned back toward the wall.

"Yo," Alex pleaded. "You said your mom is old and lives on social security. If she got sick, you could lose your kids. You can't let them be split up and placed in foster homes."

Yolanda's muscular body flew off the bed before Alex could take her next breath. She twisted Alex's orange top around her neck and raised her skyward. Alex sucked in her last breath of air.

"Dat ain't happenin'," she croaked. "Ain't nobody takin' my kids."

Their eyes met and Yolanda realized her victim's eyes were bugging out. She relaxed her grip and let Alex's feet touch concrete.

Alex rubbed her throat and carefully looked back into Yo's eyes. Tears were covering the surface like thin ice on a lake in November. Alex thought about grabbing and hugging her, but the vision of her own boobs and butt rearranged into a cheap Picasso imitation stopped her short.

Alex backed away a foot or two and growled out of her slightly damaged vocal chords. "Jake already talked to your mom and she's willing to tell the Judge that your husband beat you that night. She thinks you need to be with your kids."

Yolanda sunk to her bunk and dropped her face in her hands. She mumbled, "Momma ain't told one lie in her whole life."

Alex hesitated for just the right amount of time to get the full-blown vision of her innermost organs splattered around the cell and then gently lowered herself onto Yo's bunk. Her hand hesitantly moved to Yo's shoulder.

"Ma' kids, ah killed for ma' kids. He was beatin' all of us and now they'll be all alone." She broke down in a mixture of barks and sobs.

Hours later that night, Alex whispered, "Do you ever miss sex?"

Silence, then, "Don't know about you, Alex. Are you a lezbo or somethin'?"

"No, shit no, I just wonder if the other women in here are suffering from deprivation when I don't miss it."

"Ain't never had sex that wasn't rough or abusive, so, no, I don't miss it."

"Me neither, you know those jokes about, pull my nighty down when you're finished. I felt sorry for women when they came out with Viagra. More of them would have to lie awake, every night, waiting for their husband's magic to appear or disappear.

"I ain't listenin' to you, Alex. Now, shut up and go to sleep or you'll need another new roommate."

Alex fell asleep smiling, finally feeling secure.

40

"When I was home, I was in a better place."
Shakespeare, As You Like It

JANE

They drove through the gradual curves on a road lined with towering pines, occasionally braking for stray deer darting from one side of the road to the other. Jake glanced at Jane.

"Driving up here at dusk is the equivalent of a demolition derby. I swear those deer are trying to run into us," he muttered.

Jane's gaze focused straight ahead. Without turning, she whispered, "If the gun wasn't near the house or on the grounds, what would I have done with it? If I were Alex and thought I had just shot someone, what would I have done with the weapon?" She turned slowly and again whispered, "I would have gotten rid of it as soon as possible." She stared hard at Jake.

Their tongues touched their upper teeth at the exact moment they spoke the word in unison, "The lake."

"Oh, God, get me to a phone that works," Jake groaned. "And, as long as I'm begging, please don't let anyone stop by Paul's house before dawn."

They checked into a log-sided motel and Jake practically ran to the room. He sprinted to the phone and began pounding in Vic's numbers.

"Vic, we have a major break, but we need money." Silence, then, "It's in the lake, Vic. I'm positive. If you've ever trusted my intuitions, this is the time." Longer silence. "Vic, it won't wait 'til spring. The lakes don't thaw until May. Judge Manning is not going to be reelected and we need him to rule on this specific case." Jake emitted an exasperated sigh.

"No, everyone has to be here by 8:00. No later. Forensics, ballistics, everyone. Wait, call Charlie Decker, he can cover, damn near, everything. He's a real one-man show, but have him bring an assistant for verification and possible testimony. Vic, I'll handle the dive team. I'll coordinate with Chief Norris. Just authorize the funds. I know Medicine Lake can't swing it in their budget."

Jake put the phone down quietly and faced Jane.

"According to Vic, the dive team is going to cost big dollars, especially, because the lake is frozen. They'll need double dive teams for warm-up time, a safety diver, extra men on the safety line, chain saws and ice augers. They'll need a warm changing station, extra warm gear, full-face masks, you name it. We can't authorize turning up the heat in Paul's place without Pat's permission and we can't compromise Charlie's antiseptic search area.

"No problem," Jane replied. "We get a heated van with a place to store their equipment and change cloths. Their gear probably has to stay warm too, right?"

"I need a shower to clear my head, Jane. Hold that thought. I'm glad you're here," and he squeezed her hand.

When Jake emerged from the bathroom, Jane was already under the covers. He switched on the TV and quickly hit up arrows for volume. A news bulletin interrupted the local programming with a headline story that included video footage of Judge Manning, his daughter and the entrance to the hospital.

"Was that Judge Manning?" asked Jane, one open eye straining toward the TV.

"Sure was. How did those cameramen arrive in time to shoot film of the Judge's daughter?"

"Right." Jane looked confused and troubled. "It's not like they hang out at the hospital twenty-four hours a day."

They sat in silence as the commentator explained that Jenny had overdosed on drugs and was reported to be in a coma.

"More flames for his personal little hell." Jake sighed and draped his arm around Jane's shoulder. They stared at the screen, transfixed with the flickering light changes. Eventually they slid downward, adjusted their bodies back to back and silently waited for sleep to come.

41

"We are never so happy or unhappy as we imagine."
La Rochefoucauld, Maxims

ALEX

Syd sat in the visitor center waiting for Alex to appear. The door slid open and Bertha led a girl, with short dark hair, across the room. When they were very close, Syd suddenly recognized the even smile of Alex.

"I decided to go "butch," she grinned.

"I wouldn't make jokes about that subject in here, Alex. You could end up with a pretty full schedule. How the hell did you get a 'beauty pass?'"

"Bertha sat in my cell with her borrowed, round-tipped scissors and watched and laughed as I hacked the heck out of it."

"I wanted to see how you were doing. Jane's up north with Jake checking out Paul's place. I hate to say this, but it looks like prison life suits you. You are looking good, girl. And the change came from . . . . ?"

My little guardian angel, Jane. She shared Yolanda with me and I'm not scared twenty-four hours a day anymore," Alex replied.

"Jane said Yolanda actually listened to Mindy. She trusted her character assessments."

"God, I wish I could read people like Jane and Mindy could. Well, whatever the combination it took, she was right. Yo is extremely funny and Jane knew I would need someone strong to help me keep my sanity." Alex smiled.

Jane said it was only from watching us with our friends. She said she would love to have another man in her life but not without a network of girlfriends. She wanted me to tell you that Jake thinks he can help Yolanda. He says it's a question of self-defense versus pre-meditated murder and he's working the angles. He is such a great guy, Alex. He's totally free of pre-judgments and genuinely concerned with helping the underdogs."

Alex gave Syd a warm, knowing look. "Give Jane a huge hug and tell her I'm really happy for her."

"What do you mean, happy for her?" Syd asked in confusion.

"Open your eyes, Syd. He's mad about Jane and I'm sure she feels the same about him." Alex laughed aloud.

Syd smiled back and thought that laugh was the greatest sound she'd heard throughout this completely horrible year.

42

"It was wonderful to find America, but it would have been
more wonderful to miss it."
Mark Twain, Pudd'nhead Wilson's Calendar in Pudd'nhead Wilson

The JUDGE

The Judge waited for sleep to come, but when its arrival was two hours
overdue, he turned on the lamp and picked up the phone. He dialed the
Assistant DA and when Kenny answered, the Judge apologized for the
late hour and explained that it was urgent. Could Kenny send someone
over to the phone company as soon as possible? He'd meet them there
with specific instructions.

He rifled through his briefcase and withdrew legal forms, filled them
out and signed them. He quickly dressed and headed toward the garage. He
backtracked and went to the kitchen. There, he left a brief note. "Margaret,
I'll be back by morning and we'll go to the hospital to visit our little girl.
Thank you for being here, James."

His drive to the center of town was so preoccupied with thoughts of
Jenny that he couldn't have replayed the route if his life depended on it. It
was almost as if someone was running old home movies in his head. Jenny
at the beach, age five. Jenny, next to the Christmas tree, age six. Jenny's
graduation from eighth grade, looking like an angel in her white dress.

Jenny's first prom, looking like a hooker in a strapless red dress. Was that Clare's choice? He wondered.

He slowed the Mercedes at the front of the phone company and was surprised to see that Kenny, himself, had shown up. He grabbed the briefcase and strode across the street.

"Here's the search warrant. I brought my laptop. Meet me across the street at the coffee shop when you're finished. I need to know what you find out, tonight."

"Judge, I'm not sure this is completely legal. I mean the phone calls are confidential." Kenny whined.

"We have a search warrant for a list of phone calls. We're not listening to the calls."

The wait was excruciating and three cups of coffee had the Judge's skin crawling. He was a human vibrator by the time Kenny crossed the street with a handful of papers.

"Here it is, Judge. Complete phone records to the TV station from nine to eleven, Thursday night. Give me your laptop and we'll cross-reference."

The Judge slid the laptop across the red, vinyl tablecloth. He peered over Kenny's shoulder and watched as Kenny connected to the police web. One by one, Kenny eliminated numbers from the list.

On the thirty-first number, Kenny's eyes went wide and he turned toward the Judge. "Damn, this call came from that crazy guy's house."

"What crazy guy?"

"The guy that's been in all the papers. The guy with the property that turns out to be a forty-acre cemetery."

"David Barkley?" The Judge asked.

"Yeah, the number matches, but that's way too weird, 'cause he's in jail." Kenny stared at the number on the screen.

"Keep these pages, Kenny and thank you for coming out tonight. I don't think I've ever thanked you before, for anything, and I'm real sorry about that."

Kenny watched the blue Mercedes disappear and a strange thought crossed his mind. "Maybe that old asshole wasn't a total loser. Too bad, because he'll never get re-elected."

43

JANE

Jake skipped a shower and shave to wait for Vic's call. As he gulped his coffee and paced the small room, the local news droned from the TV.

"It looks like Judge Manning won't be re-elected." The newscaster's nasal voice was spouting out negative nothings about the Judge's daughter. Jake glanced toward the TV and saw a slender blonde with large square teeth that would have been more suitable in a cow's mouth. He strained his ears and decided she didn't have a cold; she just looked like she was sniffing something nasty.

Her irritating voice droned on, "Many local people are questioning why the Judge delivered such harsh sentences to anyone doing exactly what his daughter had did."

The phone rang and Jake lunged for it. Jane was still in the shower and they only had thirty minutes before the police chief would be in his office.

"Vic, thank goodness. What's lined up so far?"

A knock on the door interrupted the call. "Hold on, Vic."

Jake opened the door and faced two, short, bow-legged, balding men. The paunchy little men looked like miniature coat trees. The "trees" had camera bags and lenses dangling from every visible appendage, not to mention the additional bags scattered around their legs and feet.

"Shit, I had to pay the cabbie extra for all my stuff. This'll cost your firm too, Hartnett," Charlie growled.

"Come in; leave your stuff out there. I'll help in a minute, but I'm on the phone." Jake picked up the receiver and grinned, "Charlie and his assistant are here. Thanks, Vic. Give him the directions to Paul's and we'll meet him there later. I have to leave to catch Chief Norris."

Jake handed the phone to Charlie but wondered if everything was really under control. If Charlie didn't get lost, he'd have the bullet safely extracted and studied before the Chief's incompetent sidekick would be on the premises. By then, the dive team would be there and it would be too late to cancel or change those plans.

Jane emerged from the bedroom like a spotlight in a darkened theater. She was wearing her newly purchased, pink, Goodwill parka and Levis. Her curls dangled freely from beneath a bright pink, braided, ski cap and her smile warmed Jake enough to eliminate the negative thoughts he associated with the day's agenda. They grabbed each other's hands and the incongruous couple moved toward the door. Their sixteen-inch difference in height, accentuated from the rear, gave the appearance of father and small child.

"Wait." Jake reached into his suitcase and pulled out a bottle of Cognac.

"Overkill for breakfast, I'd say." Jane laughed.

"If nothing else, we can keep Stuart on his back and out of the way."

They got into the Jeep and headed to the local police shop creating imaginary "Stuart Episodes," in route.

By the time they arrived, they were hysterical, but secretly hoping nothing they had imagined would actually take place.

Their entrance was abrupt and Stuart all but raised his hands in surrender. He turned, placed one hand on his heart and gushed, "My Lord, you startled me. The Chief is already gone for the morning. What do you need?"

Jake handed Stuart the Cognac and wished him a 'Merry Christmas'.

"Ain't never heard of Cognac. Any good?"

Jake smiled and explained that it was generally drunk "straight-up" with lunch and he hoped Stuart would enjoy it.

Back in the Jeep, Jane said, "That was cruel. He'll have a snoot full by 1:00."

"Yeah, but his mental capacity won't be diminished," Jake smirked. "Now, where the hell is Chief Norris?"

44

"All clues and no solutions. That's the way things are."
Dennis Potter, The Singing Detective

JAKE

Jake murmured, "Oh shit," through clenched teeth as he recognized Chief Norris' rusty, old Suburban.

Paul's driveway swarmed with cars and men in parkas. Jake moved toward the Chief and Jane followed, slightly distracted by the divers and their van. She glanced toward the lake where she saw several, bulky figures staring at the new, first hole in the lake's surface. The sound of a chain saw wound down like a toy with a dying battery.

"Thought you'd, at least, have the courtesy to call me," the Chief accused.

"We stopped at your office first thing this morning. I didn't think you got there before 8:30," Jake replied in defense.

"This is a small town and there were at least three calls reporting headlights leaving Paul's driveway last night. Got here around 8:15 and all these vans started pulling in. What the hell is all this commotion about?"

Jake drew the Chief's arm in his and headed to the lake, in an attempt to give Charlie Decker a little more time to acquire the imbedded bullet.

He explained his theory that the gun had been disposed of in the lake and, more specifically, that the search would not cost Medicine Lake Township a cent.

Billows of vapor formed around every mouth on the lake, as if they were chain smoking. Arms flapped around shoulders, beating false warmth into their bodies, as they watched two divers immerse and emerge from the frigid ice-hole. No one was speaking and as the fourteen long minutes reached the quarter hour mark, the divers crawled out of the icy water for the last time and moved stiffly to their warm van.

Before the next two divers had a chance to get suited up, Jake speculated on his view from land to lake. There were thick, leafless bushes directly in front of the diver's hole and he wondered why they drilled and chain-sawed there. Off to the right, it was completely open to the lake. Alex wouldn't have gone through dense brush to get to the lake. He strode to the van and cautioned the next two divers to hold up until he called them.

Back at the lake, he coughed out new directions to the local men as the sub-zero air tore at his lungs. His ears had a strange, sharp tingle, as if matches were held to them and his fingers felt arthritic. He was losing the enthusiasm he felt on the Miami investigation. The locals fired up their ice augers in his pointed direction. The chain saws burst into their annoying, irregular pitches and within minutes, there was a new, three-foot square in the fifteen-inch ice.

The first of the divers sunk out of sight, through what had been beautiful blue waves of water only three months ago. The freezing Minnesota temperatures kept the diver's assistants busy, scooping new ice from the hole.

Ten, rubber-soled boots circled the hole like spokes on a wagon wheel. If the divers had looked up, rather than down, they would have seen a brown and black kaleidoscope around their only entrance to the oxygen-enriched world that could sustain them. The first hole had already frozen over.

The circle of curious, freezing men, stared at the hole. "Damn, freezin' my butt off, here," complained one.

"Yeah, better than freezin' your dick off down there," someone countered.

Occasional waves of muffled thunder rolled below the ice as the lake continued to freeze itself in the arctic temperature. The wind blew long streaks of snow over the ice in writhing strings. It looked as if fifty-foot, white snakes were slithering toward the shivering men.

Another five minutes passed when they felt a tug on the rope. As they reeled it into a mound on the ice, the diver drew closer. Before his head was visible, his outstretched arm extended and he thrust a fishing net through the icy hole. Everyone gaped at the .22, trapped like a fish.

Jake watched as Chief Norris directed its placement into a plastic bag. When Jake was positive no human hands had touched the object, he quickly turned to Paul's house.

Jane was huddled on Paul's steps, hugging herself like a small child. She looked up and blurted, "Charlie threw me out. I wasn't in the way and I wasn't talking."

"Ah, Jane, that's just Charlie. He prefers to work alone and, I promise you, nothing will be contaminated. He never screws up and isn't that what you want for Alex?"

She faced him with a look of hope and pain. "I just want it over. I want Alex out and maybe no one else in. I want peace and normality for once." Her eyes glistened.

"Don't cry, Jane," Jake teased. "Your eyes will freeze shut." He gently lifted her by one arm and turned to the house. He squeezed her shoulders with the one huge arm wrapped around her and opened the door with the other.

"Shit, Charlie, you guys are slower than the diving team. Are you losing your touch?" He challenged.

"Better be a .22 you're looking for, 'cause that's what we've got here and it's a real distinctive looking bullet. There's only one like this. Even the water and drywall damage from a year can't conceal this mark." Charlie turned and grinned, a crooked little smile that radiated satisfaction. He toddled over to Jake dangling the plastic bag with the bullet in it, as if he were the triumphant dwarf in a battle against the giants. Dwarfs forty-nine, giants zero, with no fouls or penalties.

"Even better," he smirked. "The trajectory was a straight line from the exterior door and the bullet didn't hit a damn thing before it imbedded in this cove. Hell, I never would have looked here. The drywall was such a decomposing mess, you'd have thought it was bat shit," and then he really chuckled. "Even Harry, here, wouldn't stick his hand in there. Hey, Harry, did you get that on film?"

He looked up at Jake. "I'll need a few more tests in the lab to tie it to a particular .22, but we've got such a unique marking, it'll be like finding the difference between Dolly Parton and Kate Hudson."

Charlie linked arms with his partner and he and Harry did a little dance with their short arms excitedly pumping up and down. "Go dwarfs."

45

"Nothing in his life became him like the leaving it."
Shakespeare, Macbeth, I, iv

STUART

Stuart spun the Chief's chair around a few times before settling in with his feet propped on the desk. He could get used to this office and this chair. He knew his turn would come.

The sound of the phone startled him and he wished for the millionth time that he wasn't such a jumpy person. He even panicked at his own reflection in an unexpected mirror. Someday he would have a chance to prove his courage to himself and everyone else.

The desk clerk was at lunch so Stuart picked up the call. Judge Manning explained that he had information regarding a call to the hospital and that the call came from David Barkley's house. Could Stuart, please, relay the message to Chief Norris as soon as possible? Stuart reassured the Judge that he was competent at delivering messages, hung up the phone and grabbed his coat. He neglected to leave a message for the desk clerk.

He buckled the seat belt in Medicine Lake's only squad car and headed east to David's place. His thoughts raced. "If I can pull this off, everyone will realize I should be the next chief. I mean, when Chief Norris leaves or dies, whatever."

He pictured himself in a black leather jacket with the chief's badge pinned to the pocket. He saw himself sitting in the chief's office, buzzing the desk clerk. The images swirled as he maneuvered the winding curves of the back roads.

He pulled into David's driveway and focused on the telephone number inked into the palm of his left hand. It was smudged, but legible. All he had to do was question David's wife. She would know who had called the hospital with the prophetic information that Jenny overdosed. He reveled in his anticipated success and a huge, spaced-tooth grin widened his chipmunk cheeks.

He slowed the cruiser to a halt near the detached garage and glanced toward the house. The only car in sight was a red Firebird. The silence unnerved him, but he was determined to succeed with his only challenge in ten years.

He knocked on the door, no answer. He cursed himself for not checking records before he left the office. Did David's wife work and where? What age were David's kids and were they in school? Then, he heard a motor coughing its way to a start. Stuart walked toward the sound of the, now running, engine. It sounded like a front-end loader.

The brush and woods grew thicker and darker but he followed a path. He had gone about a quarter of a mile when something heavy hit the backs of his knees. He was dropping to the ground when another blow caught the side of his head. A thin boy with bleached hair, gelled to a point on his forehead, jumped onto Stuart's stomach and held a knife to his throat.

"What do you want?" the scrawny, potential assassin demanded.

"I, I just needed to check some phone records, but no one was at the house," Stuart whispered. Panic strangled his voice along with the weight of the knife against his neck.

"So you can use them against my dad? You asshole cops are all alike." The boy exerted more pressure on Stuart's neck.

"Ddddon't do anything stupid, son." Stuart stammered.

But, before he could finish his sentence, he saw the boy's arm fly skyward. There was a splash of wet on his cheek and red droplets on his glasses. He tried to speak, but his voice was only a guttural, gurgling sound. It was impossible to suck in the air that was necessary to force out a word.

"Yyyou," and everything started to spin. The boy's face was growing and shrinking, fading from color to black and white. Only the boy's toothy grin shone out of the silhouette of his head, which was now growing dimmer. Stuart was losing consciousness.

The last recollection he had was of cold, black dirt striking his red-stained glasses.

46

"Natural forces within us are the true healers of disease."
Hippocrates, Aphorisms

The JUDGE

The Judge removed his glasses and rubbed his eyes. Chief Norris should have returned his call by now. What the hell was going on in that hick, northern town? He dialed the Chief's office one more time and the desk clerk informed him that neither the Chief nor his deputy had called in yet. She would keep trying to reach them on their cell phones. Yes, she had the Judge's number.

"Yeah, right," the Judge said aloud. "Cell phones, like they really work up there. They're lucky they've got TV the few times they can receive the satellite signals through all the damn trees."

It was almost 7:00 a.m. and Margaret would be arriving soon. His phone rang. He left the pacing circuit he'd been on since 5:00 a.m. and dove for the ringing object. Jenny's doctor wanted to see him.

He was backing the Mercedes out of the driveway when Margaret turned in.

"Jump in," he ordered.

As they drove the fifteen-minute trip to the hospital, he explained as much as he could about the phone call to the TV station and his four-hour wait to hear from Chief Manning. He knew his nerves were riding a very fine line between exhaustion and breakdown. One second his thoughts were on Jenny, and then they jumped to fat-ass Clare or David Barkley. The thoughts he couldn't control were the swimming faces of people who had appeared before him in his "joke" court, as Jenny had, so bluntly, put it. People, whose faces and voices ran together in a low-pitched, constant murmur for his attention. "Help me, please, I'm not guilty." They were chanting now, "Not guilty, not guilty, not guilty."

Margaret leaned over and touched his arm. "Judge, can you hear me?"

He glanced sideways, looked ahead again and pulled the car to the side of the road.

He slowly turned towards her, eyes glistening. "Help me, Margaret. I can't shut out the voices. They all need me."

She brought his head to her shoulder. "And you'll be there for them. Focus on Jenny right now and afterwards you can handle all of the voices, one at a time. It took this much time for them to catch up with you and it will take time to put them all to rest."

Minutes passed before a small semblance of composure returned. He put the car in gear and they continued the trip in silence. The difference, now, was the reassuring pat, pat, pat of Margaret's hand on his knee. He felt like an adolescent, beginning a new journey toward manhood only, this time, in the company of what he thought was a good, if not lucky, choice. Margaret calmed him.

When they entered the hospital, Margaret introduced herself to the doctor who immediately took her arm and began explaining the small change in Jenny's progress. She had made it through the convulsions and after less than twenty-four hours, she was showing intermittent signs of eye movement. She was trying to come out of the coma, but she was still on life support.

Margaret looked up at the doctor and words were unnecessary. His eyes met hers and he said, "Yes, I think it would be a good thing for you to be in there with her."

47

"He hath joined the great majority."
Petronius, Satyricon

STUART

The chief burst through the department's door and barked, "Where's Stuart?"

Jake followed, filling the majority of available space. When Jane entered, there was no room to turn around. The desk clerk's confused, open-mouthed stare at the three of them replaced her initial mild bewilderment.

"Where's Stuart?" the chief repeated.

"I don't know what the hell is going on around here," she replied. "There's Cognac on Stuart's desk and no note as to where he went. No note from you either, Chief and Judge Manning has called three times. Is something weird going on in Medicine Lake?"

The chief bolted toward his office. He dialed Judge Manning's number, motioned for Jake to have a seat and waited as the message machine repeated the Judge's alternate numbers. He re-dialed and got the Judge's voice mail.

His face reflected the urgency of the recorded message. He scribbled something and when he hung up his gaze fixed on what he wrote. "Care to be a temporary deputy in Medicine Lake?"

"Whatever it takes," Jake responded.

The threesome jumped into the chief's Suburban. Jake reached out the passenger window and placed the flashing light on the roof. With the lights and car spinning around the long curves, they drew closer to David Barkley's little cemetery.

Darkness was weaving itself through the dim light that outlined the house and garage. There was one light in the window nearest the wooden porch. A red Firebird sat in front of the garage. They peered through the garage window and saw the outline of a sedan, not an ordinary sedan, but one with police lights perched on a rack. The chief turned and drew his .45 from its holster.

The door next to the dimly lit window opened a crack and a weak, female voice whispered, "Go away, my husband's not home."

"It's Chief Norris and I need to talk to you."

"Go away. I've had enough intruders."

"Can't do that M'am," he replied. "My deputy was here today and we need to talk." The door opened a little wider and a mop of dyed, red hair filled the opening.

"I was at work all day and I don't know if anyone was here," she responded

"Were your kids here?"

"They were both in school," she guessed.

"Are they here now?" The chief persisted.

"My daughter's in bed." A spiral of bleached, blonde hair emerged from behind her and the mouth below it spit verbal abuses at Chief Norris.

"What the hell do you want, you son of a bitch? You want to mess up my dad some more?"

"Tommy, stop it. Shame on you."

"You ain't got the balls to stop these assholes from framing my dad," he accused.

The door opened wider and she motioned for them to come in. Tommy leapt to the door and pushed against it, while kicking at his mother. He emitted a string of curses.

"We need to look around. Jane, can you go through phone records and bills with Mrs. Barkley while we check around outside?"

Jane was still leafing through an unpaid stack of bills six inches deep when the door flew open and Chief Norris blurted, "Call 911 and White Fish Emergency. We'll be bringing Stuart in ASAP. Have the EMT's meet us at the intersection of Highways 38 and 2.

They had only been on the road for five minutes when Stuart's shallow pulse disappeared. He had lost too much blood and no amount of CPR could have brought life back to his oxygen-deprived brain.

48

"Every soul is a melody which needs renewing."
Stephane Mallarme, Crise de vers

The JUDGE

Margaret held the Judge's hand as they silently sat and watched Jenny's face. Her eyelids were twitching as if straining to stretch invisible glue. Her pale lips were also fighting the adhesive. She was attempting to break free from her self-inflicted restraints. Occasionally a small finger would snap out at the air and then slowly retreat to the sheets.

"Shouldn't we try to call Clare?' Margaret asked.

"She's already left for Europe," the judge stated. "She couldn't get refunds on the damn airline tickets. I don't even have the name of the hotel she's staying at. She left a note saying she'd call me when she arrived in Paris."

A nurse entered the room and whispered in the Judge's ear. "I'll be right back, Margaret. I have to take a call. Come out and get me if there's any change. He rushed to the front desk and picked up a receiver. Static, no sound, except crackling. "Hello," he repeated. He heard half-words, unintelligible and more crackling, finally a distant click.

He heard sirens; helicopter blades churned the air and finally the emergency doors slid open. A covered body on a stretcher whisked through, followed by a giant of a man, a small woman and Medicine Lake's Chief of Police.

"Judge," bellowed the chief. "You called my office and I tried to reach you from my cell . . . ."

The Judge interrupted, "I've been trying to reach you all day. The phone company's records listed a call from David's house to the TV station on the night I brought Jenny to the hospital. The caller gave them advance notice that she'd be coming in to the hospital. Not only coming in, but also suffering from a drug overdose. How could he have made that call when you have him in custody?"

The chief glanced from the Judge to Jake and then to Jane.

"The little foul-mouthed twerp," she accused, her voice cracking.

She stared, wide-eyed at Jake.

"She's right," Jake agreed. "We may have two serial killers here. A psychopathic adult and his genetically disturbed son. I'd be willing to bet the farm that David doesn't know all the victims in his cemetery."

A doctor appeared and rested his hand on the chief's shoulder. "We couldn't save him, I am so sorry."

Tears welled in the chief's eyes and a guttural sound replaced words. He cleared his throat, paused and said, "Stuart could barely find his own way home; he was out of his depth in a wading pool." Then he cried.

The Judge felt a hand on his shoulder and was relieved to look away from the chief. Margaret looked up at him with a mixture of promise and gratitude. "Jenny spoke your name," she said. "She's repeating daddy over and over."

The Judge spun around, grabbed Margaret's hand and sprinted to Jenny.

49

"Conscience is the perfect interpreter of life."
Karl Barth, The Word of God and the World of Man

The JUDGE

He stood on the steps in front of the courthouse surrounded by the press, suffocated by the reporters, cameras and microphones that encircled him.

He had to face this moment. All of his mistakes and shortcomings magnified, soon to be in bold print for the public to read. The culmination of every bad choice he had ever made was, now, a huge inverted pyramid that signified his start and finish. The teetering weight at the top seemed to sway on the puny foundation of his well-intended start.

He felt himself sway under the burden of confession. The bright lights and loud voices were summoning him.

"Judge, what do you intend to do about those sentences?" yelled one reporter.

"Yeah, so unlike your daughter's," screamed another.

"You screwed up my son's life," accused a bystander as he grabbed a local newswoman's microphone. "What are you gonna' do about it?"

The Judge raised his hands in submission. When the noise slightly subsided he faced the crowd and lowered his head. The noise level dropped again. He couldn't speak. Finally, in silence, he slowly raised his head. Tears filled his eyes and he spoke softly.

"I know you all have children and jobs and somehow you handled both. I failed. When I first started practicing law, my only goal was to serve justice. I wanted equality and a fair justice system. As the years passed, I clung to that dedication, neglecting my family. Then, my only child began a descent toward the lows of society and I lost the vision of my direction. I didn't know how to cope with the worry, the sleepless nights, or the discipline. All I felt was the enormous love of a parent, a parent that would do anything for the survival of their pup; even the worst pup."

He hesitated and continued in a shallow voice. "I know you can't forgive me for the wrongs I've done, but in the time I have left in office, I will review every case and bring each one to the public's attention. If I can redo anything I overlooked, I will do it."

"I don't expect to be re-elected and if you ask me to resign right now, I will, but I would appreciate the chance to correct my mistakes. My office will provide an email address and you can send your personal stories to me. I'm spending all of my time at the hospital with my daughter, but as soon as I can bring her home, I'll also leave my home phone number."

"I sincerely apologize to all the people I have hurt. I am truly sorry, but right now, I do not think I can survive without my daughter. She is my life. I just want a second chance to be a good father."

At the end of his statement, he pinched the bridge of his nose, shook his head and turned away from the cameras. He struggled up the steps, as if he had aged twenty years in twenty-four hours, and disappeared into the courthouse. An hour later, he left his chambers, drained and out of tears and prayers. He had just lost his beloved career, his wife and home, but as he drove to the hospital he thought, "If Jenny lives, I don't care."

50

"I shall temper justice with mercy."
John Milton, Paradise Lost

YOLANDA

The courtroom was unusually quiet. Jane and Jake were whispering softly in a corner. The District Attorney was shuffling the papers that made the only sound in the room. Yolanda's court appointed attorney sat at her left and his appearance would prove to be a mere formality.

Yolanda's mother sat close enough to rest her hand on her daughter's shoulder. A doctor and three nurses whispered earnestly behind them.

The Judge cleared his throat and the paper shuffling and whispers ceased. "As I promised in my press conference, I will be re-examining many of my prior cases. This particular case seemed to warrant my immediate attention."

His gaze rested on Yolanda's scarred face. His eyes and voice softened. "Yolanda. It seems as though I overlooked many important pieces of evidence during your trial. I sincerely apologize."

"The police have provided arrest records that prove your husband was a life-long alcohol and drug abuser. The drug abuse included both cocaine and heroin, very expensive habits. I'm certain these addictions made any semblance of normal, family life impossible. I can only imagine the strain it put on you and it seems as though I've put additional strain on you, your mother and children."

The doctors have testified that you were in the emergency room on several occasions, due to your husband's abuse. He directed his gaze to the doctor and nurses. "Would any of you care to add anything that might not be included in the hospital records?"

"I would," said a short, gray-haired nurse. She stood and hesitated for a moment. "The hospital records eliminate all emotion and opinions. I have worked the emergency room for over twenty years and I've never seen anyone in Yolanda's condition, nor have I seen anyone survive that condition. We've never seen a fighter like Yolanda." She turned to the rest of the hospital group and they nodded their heads in unison. "We could have used a sewing machine to close up all of her wounds. She needed over two hundred stitches to close her husband's slashes and they were not superficial wounds. He cut through muscles and severed an artery. She had intestinal damage and her heart stopped beating, twice, during surgery. We have also set broken bones on two of her children. That man deserved to die."

"This isn't a question of his deserving to die," the Judge admonished. "It's a question of whether Yolanda murdered him. The photographs you provided confirm that Yolanda suffered a horrible beating and the records of your service confirm that she would not have survived without you. My question is, did she murder him or did she protect herself and her children when she returned home that night?"

The Judge directed his attention to Yolanda's mother and he saw her faltering gaze avert his eyes. An inappropriate surge of pleasure swept through him. He had a dim recollection of the gift he possessed in his earlier years on the bench. He sensed her fear. Not fear of him, not fear for her daughter, but the innermost struggle of an honest woman hesitating to speak a lie.

The Judge, once again, cleared his throat, but rather than asking her the direct question she feared, he said, "I have new evidence that Yolanda's mother was watching the children the night of Yolanda's release from the hospital. Yolanda's husband attacked her the moment she entered the house. Because of this information, I am reversing my previous ruling.

His death was the result of self-defense. If there are no further questions, Yolanda is free to leave."

The District Attorney stood dumbfounded while everyone else in the room hugged. Even the doctor and nurses were cheering. Yolanda hugged her mother tightly and wept.

Jane waited her turn and when, at last, Yolanda released her mother, Jane whispered, "Enjoy some time with your mom and children. Then, please call me. We have to talk to Alex and her sister."

51

"You and me, we've made a separate peace."
Ernest Hemingway, In Our Time

The JUDGE

Margaret was preparing dinner and the Judge was sitting next to the island watching her hands deftly roll and flour, slice and dice, as if she had three pairs of them. All the while, she was humming or smiling and pointing out the culinary triumphs that were Jenny's favorites.

Jenny was resting, peacefully, upstairs and they would join her soon for their shared dinner and nightly conversations. Some evenings the Judge would answer his emails while they watched the big screen TV the Judge had bought for her. He justified the purchase by reminding himself it would be the last extravagance prior to selling their monstrosity of a house.

As soon as Jenny fully recovered, they would find a smaller house and cars. Margaret had already begun filling the garage for the auction. The Judge hoped the proceeds could make up the difference between the mortgage and the lesser amount of what the house was actually worth.

He promised himself that they would never downsize to the point of losing their cook and friend, Margaret.

The only cloud that followed him from room to room was that of Clare's puffy, white face. He explained to Margaret and Jenny that Clare never called him from Paris. He had the police tracking the airlines, her pre-purchased tickets and the hotels she preferred to stay in, but as of today, they had no information.

"Daddy," Jenny paused, for over a minute. The doctors told him that Jenny would experience these lulls in memory and speech for up to a year. She still needed therapy and lots of rest.

"Daddy, I was thinking how nice it is, not to have momma around. Didn't her voice and her schedules ever make you crazy?"

He smiled. "Oh, honey, she meant well." Then, he chuckled. "Actually she drove me, damn near, insane."

Margaret said, "Shame on you two. You'll be missing her soon."

The Judge smiled at Jenny and in unison, they giggled, "Don't think so."

52

"Here's the smell of the blood still.
All the perfumes of Arabia will not sweeten this little hand."
William Shakespeare, Macbeth

The CHIEF

Jake and Jane were perched on opposite ends of the Chief's desk. The Judge and Chief Norris occupied the only chairs in the tiny office.

"Something is extremely strange about that boy," the Judge warned. "When I parked out front today, I saw the red Firebird and suddenly remembered Jenny coming home, in a car that was its twin, the night she overdosed. When we got the records from the phone company we found out the call, announcing Jenny's arrival at the hospital, came from David's house. Impossible since you had David locked up in here. I think the kid is involved."

"I do, too," offered Jake. "One of the people that went missing, three years ago, was a thirteen year old kid. What could he have done to piss off David?"

Jane scowled. "I just don't like his filthy mouth and the way he treats his mother."

Jake laughed, appreciating how good she looked in her Salvation Army sweatshirt and jeans. She was a woman who could fit comfortably into a man's budget.

"Right, Jane," Jake said. "If that was the criteria for suspicion, half the teenagers in the country would be suspects."

"I've asked Mrs. Barkley to meet with David, alone. She protested, at first, but I convinced her that questioning him in front of her son would only aggravate David's already distressed mental state. Their attorney should be here any minute."

The phone rang and the Chief grabbed the receiver. He scribbled and nodded his head several times before hanging up.

"Most of the results are in from Charlie and the forensic team. The bullet you found in Paul's ceiling matches the gun we found in the lake. More importantly, some of the prints were still intact and we have four sets of them. A single, faint print matches a local guy, named Andy. I know him and he's not a suspect. Trust me."

"Alex told us she got the gun from Andy, so it's a pretty safe bet that his prints would be on it," said Jake.

"The second prints belonged to Alex," the Chief continued.

Jane stood abruptly. "But she didn't kill him."

"Don't worry," the Chief said. "I mean, she has the infra-red evidence that corroborates her testimony. The trajectory study of the bullet matches her description of where she was standing and Charlie will testify that nothing touched the bullet before it lodged in the ceiling."

"Hold on, there's more," the Chief pressed on. "Charlie found some hairs in the hallway and the DNA matches Pat's and her prints are the third set on the gun."

"She was there." Jane's face whitened and her stomach recoiled with disappointment. She still harbored some hope that Pat wasn't involved.

"Charlie hasn't matched the fourth and most prominent set of prints. He's working on it."

"Holy shit," Jake blurted. "This is starting to sound like the shoot-out at the OK Corral. How many country cowboys tried to shoot Paul?"

The Judge stared at the floor. "How many people wanted to shoot Paul?" he repeated to himself. Probably all of them, with the exception of the one I sentenced. A slow flood of guilt reddened his face. Fortunately, there was a knock at the door.

"Let's get the show on the road," the Chief exclaimed as he recognized David's attorney. He led Jane and the Judge to the mirrored room and continued down the hall with Jake, Mrs. Barkley and her attorney.

Mrs. Barkley crossed the room and stood, silently studying David's face. "How could you, David?" Her voice came out in a high-pitched accusation.

David, finally, stopped fidgeting for the first time since his arrest. He faced the floor in the position of a small, scolded child. He sat quietly with his hands folded in his lap.

"David, answer me," her whine continued. "For God's sake, what have you done to our son?"

He brought his face up, his questioning stare locked on her face.

The Chief interrupted. "David, do you know a boy named Eddie Zinda?"

David remained focused on his wife's face, but replied with a nonchalant, "Yeah, he played soccer with my son, so what?"

"Do you know where he is now?" The Chief continued.

"Nah, their family moved away three years ago," David kept staring at his wife.

"No," said the Chief. "They moved away two years ago. One year after their son disappeared."

"Whatever." David's bored responses were about to change.

"Eddie was murdered. We found his body on your property and your son is our number one suspect," the Chief informed him.

"You son of a bitch," screamed David's wife as she flung herself at him. She fell over the attorney who scrambled to get out of her way. Jake took a giant stride and caught her by her waist. He held her flailing body while she exhausted a string of curses.

"You chose to get rich at any cost. You and your get even schemes. You've ruined our family, our lives. You've patterned our son after your own sick self. I hate you." She turned toward Jake's big chest and began sobbing with curses still trickling between the sobs.

David went pale. His attorney asked for a short recess as he righted his chair and smoothed his suit.

"I think we need some answers, David," said Jake. He led David's wife to a chair in the corner where she sat, head bobbing, while emitting high-frequency hiccups.

"David, we've got eight bodies, so far, all from your forty acres. We suspect there'll be, at least, eight more," the Chief blew air through his compressed lips. "Your son killed my deputy."

David froze, but then, his fingers moved, as if he was mentally counting. He remained silent.

When fifteen minutes passed, Jake and the Chief left the room.

53

"Fear has many eyes and can see things underground."
Cervantes, Don Quixote

ALEX

Alex felt the presence of someone at the cell door. She turned in that direction and caught the solemn expression on Bertha's face.

"What's wrong, Bertha, what's happened?"

"I tried to change the Warden's decision," Bertha said. "I really tried, Alex. I mean Yolanda's only been gone two days, but we're facing another over-crowded situation."

Her downcast eyes revealed the news Alex had been dreading. A sickening swirl of fear was flapping its wings in her head. Her brain processed the emotion and drove it through the rest of her body with the speed of a lightning bolt. Her stomach lurched and she could feel her heart thumping like a piston.

A tall figure emerged from behind Bertha. Another guard followed the dark image. Alex froze as she attached a name to the approaching face. "The Thief." That's what she was famous for in the outside world, stealing material goods. In here, she stole all that was left, a shred of dignity and self-respect.

"Bertha," Alex began, but Bertha lowered her head and turned away. The second guard pressed her remote, the cell door opened and she shoved the Thief into Alex's home.

Alex backed toward the commode and suddenly felt an urgent need for a restroom. "Oh, God," she thought. "I can't do that in front of her. Oh, God, when will I do it? Oh, God, help me, please."

"Don't look so scared, sugar," slurped the sickeningly sweet voice. "I like to take my time, get to know my newest attractions." She sat on the lower bunk. "This your bed? We could just share it, now that your big watch dog has flown the coop."

"Please, God, calm me down," Alex pleaded silently as she climbed to the top bunk.

Her heart continued to pound and she crossed her hands over her chest to keep the Thief from hearing her fear.

A guard appeared at the cell door. "You got company, Alex. I'll follow you to the Visitor Center."

As Alex stepped past the lower bunk, she heard the saccharine voice, "Just a short intermission, honey, and then it's show time."

Alex's eyes locked on the wall at the opposite end of the Visitor's Center and she seemed to be floating across the floor toward the metal tables. She heard the voices but couldn't identify their foreign language. Her confused mind sat in limbo waiting for an interpreter.

"Alex?" The sound of her own name brought her eyes down to the table.

"Alex, what the hell? You're scaring me," said Jane.

"Yeah, you's lookin' weird, Alex." Yolanda twisted her head to look up at Alex.

Alex inhaled loudly and her exhale trickled out "the Thief."

"You gots to be shittin' me," barked Yo. "Jane, go and call Jake. Ah know he can get 'dis shit changed. Ah left you too soon, Alex. You did all you could for me an' my kids, momma didn't even have to lie. Ah'd come back in here, if ah could."

Alex just stared.

Jane returned. "Jake said someone at the prison must owe the Judge a favor. He's calling him right now."

"Alex, try to talk. It'll help," Jane prompted.

"About what?" whispered Alex. "Me, turning into the 'Mouse'? You think I could ever erase that from my memory. I could never look in a mirror again."

"Ah shoulda' taken you to the weight room 'sted of that TV room," Yo said.

"Oh hell, Yo, Alex could probably take the Thief, right now," said Jane.

"You think so?" asked Yo, genuinely surprised.

Alex slowly looked up. "You think so?"

"Damn right," exclaimed Jane. "Especially if you think about the 'Mouse' being abused by all of those guys while you're pounding on the Thief."

They stalled and continued pumping Alex's ego until the last second of their visitation time. As they walked to their car Yo said, "Alex can't fight the Thief, Jane."

"She's got to believe she can, until Jake can get the Thief out of her cell. You want her to just lie there and take it?" Jane's eyes were moist and she said, "I'm afraid for her, Yo."

"Yeah, me too. Wish 'ah was still in there. Ah'd slap that bitch so hard her cousins would go unconscious."

54

The JUDGE

When the Judge received Jake's phone call, the faces began their incessant swirls in his head. "Who the hell was Alex?" he asked himself. Jake must have sensed the confusion from the Judge's hesitation.

"She allegedly shot her business partner about a year ago," Jake said.

"Right, right," responded the Judge. "But I really don't know anyone that could influence the Warden of that prison. I can't think of a soul who would take the time to change the Warden's decision on who shares cells with whom."

Jake felt deflated and the Judge felt flattened. "Allegedly shot," he said aloud when he hung up. "I sentenced her to fifty years." He could see the top of Alex's head buried in her hands. He never even got a good look at her face and he had sentenced her to fifty years in prison. "Oh, God." How long would it take him to change all of the inept sentences he delivered to so many people? The mental, self-flagellation ceased long enough for Jenny to float inside his closed eyes. Her almost healthy, smiling face danced through his thoughts. He had his daughter back and now he was finally going to try to bring all of the other families back together. Margaret would tell him to take one-step at a time. He focused again.

Jake's call prompted him to realize the urgency of re-evaluating Alex's imprisonment. He checked the Court calendar and made phone calls to set a preliminary hearing for the newest suspect, the suspect that could prove Alex innocent. He called in favors from the District Attorney and the defense lawyers. He felt a great amount of gratitude when the clerk called and told him Pat would be present for a preliminary hearing tomorrow afternoon.

He left the courthouse and drove north. The sky was a deep gray, overcast with snow laden clouds. The weatherman predicted another six inches for tomorrow. He stepped out of his Jeep, slid his hand along the door and smiled. He had finally sold the big, blue Mercedes. In fact, he had sold the pair of them to a woman who bore a striking resemblance to Clare. She had waddled up the driveway dragging her scrawny husband by the arm, repeating, "Just write the check, dear. We'll talk about this at home."

He entered the Chief's office after only a slight knock and peered at the tall man sitting across from the Chief.

"I'm sorry, I'll come back," the Judge said.

"No, Judge. Glad you stopped by. I think you should hear this," the Chief said with a confused expression.

"You know the FBI got involved in the search of Barkley's forty acre cemetery, right? Well, seems as though their investigation turned up evidence of drug dealings. One of the victims was a thirteen-year old boy. His friends have all admitted to buying marijuana from Tommy Barkley. They told the agent that they knew Tommy added slices of crack to the marijuana he sold to other people. He also sold Ecstasy. He may have added that to your daughter's drinks. You did say his red Firebird was the car she came home in, the night she overdosed, right?"

The color drained from the Judge's face. He was as white as the snow mounting on the window, building its barrier to the outside world. He stuttered, "Hhhhe almost killed her."

"I'm sorry, Judge," the Chief offered. "There's more. Since we had David locked up here when Stuart went to Barkley's house, we think Tommy killed him. Don't know if it was drug related or if he thought he was protecting his dad. Agent Morgan thinks Tommy altered Jenny's drugs to punish you, or the law through you, for locking up his dad."

The Chief added, "The FBI will be questioning Tommy tomorrow. If you want to come by and listen in, you're welcome."

"I've got a pretty important hearing in the afternoon that I can't miss. Could you tape the interview?" The Judge rose and slowly shuffled back to his car through the deepening snow. By the time he started the Jeep, it was a whiteout. He could barely see the road ahead and as the snow mounted, so did his temper.

He pulled into his garage, three-hours later, and then felt his way to the house. When he opened the kitchen door and saw Margaret moving busily through a thick aroma of roast duck, his temper dwindled to a low flame.

"They think David Barkley's son deliberately overdosed Jenny," he blurted.

Margaret reacted to his news as if she was suffocating. Her hand flew to her throat and she gasped, "But, he's just a boy."

"Guess the apple doesn't fall too far from the tree," the Judge replied.

He passed through the kitchen and headed up the stairs to Jenny's room. An hour later, the Judge knew every drug Tommy sold, everyone he sold to, and more importantly, who he bought it from. Marijuana and alcohol were the only drugs she used; she just didn't count on someone deliberately overloading hers. He was convinced that she drank the alcohol and smoked the weed in retaliation to the ridiculous life style they were living, not because she genuinely liked either one.

He felt warmth as he sat next to Jenny and realized they were actually communicating. He had never before sat and talked to his daughter.

"How did you meet Tommy?"

"He dropped out of school a year ago, but still showed up every Friday. He'd have fifteen, maybe twenty, cars full of kids buying drugs in the school parking lot. I knew he sold more than marijuana, but I never tried anything else. I'm sorry daddy, but I hated coming home. Momma had her stupid dinner parties every night and if I was drunk or stoned, I didn't have to pretend to be sick all weekend. I hated it here. Momma drove me like a circus pony."

"I think she had a couple of matching ponies," and he raised his hand and waved it in a Queen-like salute. They laughed and then hugged.

55

ALEX

Alex slowly headed back to her cell. The guard ahead of her was the hare and Alex played the tortoise role. The fear was weighing her down again. She focused on Jane and Yo telling her, with conviction, that she could defend herself against the Thief.

She got to her cell and the guard pressed the remote. The Thief was lying in the bottom bunk and she slowly patted the spot next to her, as she grinned up at Alex. The Jack O' Lantern grin with the two missing teeth sent an icy chill down Alex's back.

Alex hopped up to the top bunk and held her breath. It was almost dinner hour. If she could just last that long, there would be another temporary reprieve. As the minutes ticked by, she concentrated on controlling her breathing. Calm down, calm down, she repeated to herself.

Alex heard rustling below her and suddenly the Thief's arms were resting on the edge of her bunk and their faces were inches apart.

"So, whatcha' gonna' do without your watch dog? Did your big doggy desert you, honey?"

"You disgust me," Alex grated through clenched teeth.

"I'm gonna' show you something disgusting, you little anorexic twit," and the arms that had been leaning a moment ago, shot to Alex's throat.

Alex spun her body and kicked at the Thief's chest sending her backwards toward the sink. Her back arched, unnaturally, over the porcelain basin, but she straightened up and threw herself at Alex.

Alex kicked again and caught the Thief in her mid section. The blow went unnoticed and the Thief kept advancing. Alex started swinging and realized she had no idea of how to throw a punch. She had never struck anything, intentionally, in her whole life.

The Thief punched Alex hard in the face, then grabbed her neck and squeezed it tightly in the crook of her arm. Her free arm was pulling at Alex's baggy, orange pants.

"Oh, my God," Alex screamed and that was when Shirley, "the Mouse" appeared. Her face floated around the cell. Those huge, sad eyes were everywhere and Alex went insane. She started screaming, kicking, punching and biting. The "Mouse" floated in and out of her vision, but disappeared when Alex felt her head crack firmly on the concrete. The Thief was on top of her. Her arms were pinned and her kicking was ineffectual beneath the heavy weight.

"Get off of her. I said get the hell off of her." Bertha's normally placid face screwed into a menacing mass that conveyed the same message as a pointed gun. "Get off of her and come here." She warned, "Alex, go to the back of the cell." Bertha spoke into a black box and another guard instantly materialized behind her.

"It's all on tape, Thief, from the minute you entered this cell." Bertha held up a small recorder. She pressed the remote for the cell door and stepped back. "Let's see, does not play well with others. That should give you a few days in solitary."

The tall woman moved slowly to the door but when she was even with Bertha, she spat out, "You'll get yours. I own this place, now that Yolanda's gone." She turned to Alex and added, "Keep that bed warm, sweet thing. I'll be back."

Alex half sat and half fell into the lower bunk.

Bertha checked her bleeding nose and lip and said, "Girl, you're ok. Just rest here. I gotta' get that menace to solitary and then I'll be back to check on you. Have yourself a good cry," and she left.

Alex did cry, but not before reminding herself that Jane and Yo were wrong. She couldn't defend herself. If she remained in here, she was eventually going to die, either physically or spiritually.

56

"Injustice anywhere is a threat to justice everywhere."
Martin Luther King, letter from the Birmingham jail

PAT

She entered the courtroom in a tailored, gray suit, white blouse and pearls. She reminded herself that no matter what she was wearing today, she would eventually be dressed in a prison uniform.

She took her seat next to her attorney who whispered, "Don't offer any information. Just answer their questions with minimal wording."

Pat glanced up at him and said, "You just don't get it, do you? I told you, I'm guilty."

"There are different degrees of guilt, Pat. Trust me," he replied.

The Judge took a long, hard look at Pat, reminding himself of his past ineptitude. There would no longer be a sea of faces swimming around him; faces with no connections to the sentences he delivered. He would be certain, from now on, of each of his decisions.

Pat looked at her lap, barely seeing the Judge. Another Alex, he thought. Just put your head down and confess. His intuition had returned and he reveled in his renewed insights as well as his renewed feelings toward life, Jenny and his beloved career.

The District Attorney called Charlie to the stand. He explained all of his findings at Paul's, the gun, the bullet, the forensic and ballistic conclusions on those findings. He emphasized that three of the bullets taken out of Paul came from the gun they fished out of the lake. That same gun had Pat's fingerprints on it. The bullet found in the corner of the ceiling also matched the gun from the lake. That bullet never struck anything before it hit its final resting place.

Pat's attorney cross-examined Charlie. "Isn't it true that the bullet taken from the rotting drywall never struck anything?" Charlie nodded affirmatively. Could it then follow that it was Pat's bullet. Her fingerprints" . . . . Before he could finish, the District Attorney interrupted with an objection. "Speculation, your honor."

"Sustained," said the Judge.

"Let me re-phrase, Your Honor," said Pat's attorney. "My client's fingerprints were found on a gun, from which one bullet was fired into rotted drywall. A bullet that never struck anything. That bullet could have been the only one that Pat fired."

"Objection. Speculation," repeated the DA.

"Sustained," repeated the Judge.

"Actually," said Charlie, "There is another confessed shooter whose description of where she was standing that night, precisely matches the infrared trajectory study. It seems Alex Anderson fired the only bullet that didn't hit Paul."

"I want that stricken from the records, Your Honor, speculation on the witness' part," shouted Pat's attorney.

The Judge disregarded the commotion. That testimony was a slap in his face. Alex was innocent and he had taken a year out of her life. The years we lose in an already short life cannot be replaced. Clare had stolen most of his. He had stolen from Alex.

His attention riveted back to his courtroom. "Strike that from the record and Mr. Hiller, please, restrain yourself from offering opinions. Just answer the questions asked of you."

Beads of perspiration were visible above Pat's perfectly shaped eyebrows. Her streaked hair was becoming damp and she knew this was the moment where she had to end everything she had worked so hard to achieve. She rose and faced the Judge. "Judge, I shot Paul and there's no point in continuing the questioning."

The reporter sitting at the back of the Courtroom leapt to his feet and raced through the doors. It was less than fifteen minutes before reporters from two other TV stations circled the Courthouse.

By the time the Judge left the Courthouse, reporters from both stations and the newspaper were swarming his car.

"Judge, do you think she's guilty?"

"Sounds a lot like Alex Anderson, doesn't it, Judge?"

"When's the Jury Trial?"

He climbed into the Jeep, too tired to drive, but then he remembered his past when the fatigue stemmed from the depth of his bones. A debilitating weariness that made breathing an effort. He turned his thoughts to Jenny and Margaret and the possibility of setting all things right. He smiled and the slightly upturned corners of his mouth produced inner warmth, a new emotional balance. His aches and pains disappeared.

57

"Then words came like a fall of winter snow."
Homer, Iliad

DAVID

Jake and Jane picked up the Judge and drove north, again to Chief Norris' northern jurisdiction, David's little cemetery, the scene of Paul's death and Alex's ten year exile. The past year's occurrences had shaken the small communities. The news of finding so many of the disappeared victims had put fear into the local people. They were used to drownings, hunting accidents and snowmobile deaths but they never experienced multiple murders at this level. People were actually locking their doors.

"We've got to be back for Pat's trial tomorrow. Do you think David will talk or is this another trek back in time to a silent movie in cell block eight?" Jane asked.

"The Chief says he's going to bring in David's wife and son at the same time. Let them have at him," Jake grinned. "That amounts to one crazy chip off the old block and a screeching woman. That's enough to get a sane man chattering; like teeth at forty below zero."

"Very funny, dick-head," laughed Jane.

When they reached the station and got out of the car, the frozen snow screeched under their feet and the wind almost blew them up the steps.

They opened the police station door and a gust of white powder circled the room.

"He's waiting for you in his office," the desk clerk said, "and thanks for dusting the place."

They filed to the interrogation room. David sat silently, examining the floor with the focused intensity of a health inspector.

Jake noted that he wasn't fidgeting anymore.

"Before you bring Tommy and my wife in here, I gotta' say something," David said in a barely audible voice.

"Don't say anything," cautioned his attorney. "Just answer the questions."

"No, this can't wait. I'm almost relieved that it's over. I really screwed up my kid. You know, I did it all for him. So that he could have all the things I never had. Now, his life is as screwed up as mine. They were all such crooks, they really deserved to die."

"Who are they?" asked the Chief.

"I'll give you the names later, after I talk to Tommy," David said.

"We need to know, now, if you shot Paul," said Jake.

"Yeah, I did." David's menacing look kept his attorney quiet.

"I wanted to kill the asshole. He took over my real estate deals and started making money with the same jerks that shut me out. I went to his house that night and had a perfect bead on his forehead. He heard the car door slam at the same time I did. He kind of turned as he jumped up and my shot caught him in the shoulder. I had to get out of there before I could finish him. I saw Alex's car was parked near mine, but she was running toward Paul's house and never even looked back at me."

The Chief slid a piece of paper over to David and asked him to write down all of the names of the people he punished.

"They're not all taken care of yet," David confessed. "We had a real scam going. Sam knew what was going on and when he quit, he told Paul. Paul moved in on the two real estate offices that were making the money. He started doing appraisals for them on the vacant land they wanted to buy. When he'd bring the value in at far less than market value, their various small corporations would purchase the land, get variances from the zoning office and . . . ."

"What kind of variances?" asked the Chief.

"If it was riverfront property with 300 foot minimums, their guy in the zoning office would reduce the minimums to 100 feet. That way, they could get more riverfront lots out of the same parcel," David said. "Then they brought in the builders who were also part of the small corporations and they would build inferior quality homes and the group made even more money."

"Didn't anyone ever complain or sue them?"

Davis snorted. "Sure, but it was all kept quiet. You live here Chief and you don't know that the Judge and the DA are corporate partners. They own the local newspaper, too. No one ever won a case against them. Everyone in their little circle of thieves was getting rich, except me, so they had to slowly disappear."

"Give me a list of the people you got rid of and add the names of the people you still need to eliminate. This could really help you later on, David." The Chief exhaled loudly and tapped Jake's arm. "Let's go."

The two left the room and the Judge slowly followed. He was quietly arguing with himself. "How much could you do for children? How much is enough? Look what David thought he had done for Tommy." Finally, the slow realization hit him. It wasn't degrees of how much to give, it was setting the example. If he had gotten his life organized, Jenny's life would have been different. A decent, honest home environment would have done her more good than all of the material things. That truth existed even in David's messed up little world.

When they reached the hallway, Jake said, "I think he's telling the truth. We went through all of Paul's appraisals and he was only doing work for those two real estate offices, no banks or lending companies. Two of their sales people were found buried at David's, along with one of the brokers, some guy from the zoning office and a local builder. David was going to get them all. By the way, Alex didn't do one appraisal for either of those offices. Looks like Paul cut David's car out of the gravy train all by himself."

58

"All truth is good, but not all truth is good to say."
Anonymous (African Proverb)

The JUDGE

The media surrounded the Courthouse. Technicians were racing around adjusting microphones and lighting. The newspapers and TV stations ran the story of Pat's confession nonstop until it was picked up and syndicated nationally.

The Judge had requested a preliminary meeting in his chambers with Pat, the prosecuting attorneys and the defense attorney.

The uncomfortable silence snapped like a rubber band when the Judge asked Pat's attorney how she was going to plead.

His voice was resigned and unemotional when he replied, "Guilty of First Degree Homicide, Your Honor."

"Are you certain of this plea, Pat?" The Judge tried to find the truth in her icy blue eyes. He continued looking into them as if they were crystal balls and the image of what truly happened at Paul's place would emerge.

Suddenly, the chamber door flew open and an off-balance Bailiff banged sharply against it, struggling with the young woman he was attempting to restrain.

All heads turned in their direction and Pat gasped, "Erica."

"It's alright, Jim. Let her in," said the Judge.

"No, it's not alright," Pat sputtered.

"What are you doing, mom? Weren't you or Walt ever going to tell me? I saw you on the news last night." Erica began to cry and rushed toward her mother. They embraced and Pat fought hard to control herself. When she could speak, she said quietly, "It's all ok now, honey. It's all over with."

Erica turned to the Judge and shouted, "It's not over with. Mom didn't shoot him. I shot my father."

"Come sit here and calm down." The Judge brought a chair near his desk and patted the seat in a gesture generally reserved for a dog.

Erica moved toward him, but remained standing. Her quivering lips revealed that she was very close to tears, but her voice came out in an even, controlled volume. "Walt, my step dad, called me the morning that mom supposedly left for Missouri. He was worried because mom had been getting so many threatening letters from my dad and he was afraid that she was going to try to talk to him. That never worked, so I flew into Minneapolis and rented a car.

"Erica, honey, you don't know what you're saying." Pat went to her side and hugged her. She tried to direct her to the door, but Erica resisted, stood firmly and faced the Judge.

"When I got to my dad's, I saw mom's car next to the house and another car barely missed a tree as it turned to leave the driveway," she continued. "I ran toward the steps and when I looked down there was a gun lying there. I heard shouting, picked up the gun and looked in. My dad's shoulder was covered with blood. Mom faced him and I heard her say, 'I'll fight you, Paul, in and out of court. You are the master of putting fear into people, but I'm not afraid of you anymore.'"

"Erica, please, stop talking, please," Pat moaned.

However, Erica pushed on. "My mom turned away from dad and as she started walking toward me and the door, I saw my dad raise a gun. He had it aimed at mom's back and I went crazy. I just started shooting. I don't know how my shots missed mom. I mean, I was shaking so bad and it was all so fast and scary. I just couldn't let him shoot her. We ran out, mom grabbed the gun and threw it in the lake. We were half way home when we realized that we had made everything worse by leaving the scene. Someone else already shot him but mom was afraid I would end up in prison. We were both hoping he wasn't dead, but we left."

Erica collapsed in the chair and said, "Mom is all I have. I could never get close to dad. He had such a short temper fueled by hateful vengeance. We finally had a great life with Walt, but my dad kept threatening to get even, to ruin mom and keep us apart." She finally cried and Pat knelt next to her, smoothing Erica's hair with her hands.

"Oh, sweetie, I tried so hard to keep you out of the mess I created." Pat wept.

"The Court will recess until we have time to review this new information." The Judge walked over to Pat and Erica. As he laid his hand on Pat's shoulder, he looked at the DA, "I don't think we need to keep either woman in custody. They are not threats to society and we have no fear of their fleeing our jurisdiction. Do you agree?"

The response was a confused affirmative nod.

59

"Happiness in the ordinary sense is not what one needs in life,
though one is right to aim at it. The true satisfaction is to come through
and see those whom one loves come through."
E. M. Forster, letter in Selected Letters

ALEX

Bertha stood outside the cell and beamed with the intensity of a marquis billboard.

"Don't tell me, Bertha," said Alex. "You just won the lottery."

"Better than that, Alex. The Warden wants to see you right away." She continued to grin and pressed her remote. The cell door opened, she gave a slight bow and her hand gestured toward the exit.

"Oh, hell," cursed Alex. "It's not about another new cellmate, is it?"

Bertha shook her head negatively, the grin never leaving her face.

"The Thief choked in her sleep and I'm a suspect in foul play, right?" Alex pressed on. "Something happened to Yolanda. Something happened to Jane."

By the time they reached the Warden's office, Alex had invented fifteen possible reasons for the Warden's requested visit and the smile never left Bertha's face.

They entered the austere, cramped office and the Warden pointed to a chair for Alex. Bertha stood next to her.

"Alex, I've just received a phone call from the Governor's office. It seems that you are one of the few people in here that is, unbelievably, innocent. I have contacted your sister and she will provide a ride to wherever you feel like going. Bet that news breaks your heart, right?"

Alex inhaled deeply and fainted. When she came to, she faced a guard's shirt that appeared to contain twin beach balls. She raised her gaze and looked into Bertha's smiling face. She reached up and hugged the woman who had befriended her from her first day in hell.

Bertha led her down to the Visitor Center. Across the room Sydney, Jane and Yolanda stood in captivated silence. Alex could not move another inch. She stared at her sister and best friends, then, looked toward the exit and back at Bertha. Bertha gave her a gentle push forward, but Alex hesitated again. A scene from Butch Cassidy and the Sundance Kid flashed through her head. One more step and they'll open fire, she thought.

One year out of her life and the constraints were more normal than freedom. What had she become? She spied the metal table to her right and thought about taking a seat. She would wait, right there, for the shooters to come to her.

She slumped to the chair as the posse drew near.

"Alex, Alex," Jane shouted. "I have my job back again. I'm the new District Manager for all of Pat's health clubs.

"Yeah, an' ah'm the new trainer," grinned Yolanda. "Ah got a new plan for a kid's class. You know, fight the obese children in America stuff . . . ."

Jane interrupted. "Pat's daughter shot Paul 'cause he was aiming a gun at Pat's back. The Judge ruled it as self-defense, and, you won't believe this, the police found the Judge's wife buried on David's acreage . . . ."

"Jane, stop." Syd admonished as she watched Alex stare in a non-comprehending daze.

She slowly rounded the table's edge and touched Alex's shoulder.

"It's ok, Alex, you're ok. Look what we brought you."

Alex looked up and strained to see a little, furry head with huge, blue eyes that peered curiously through the netting of a small canvas bag.

"He's yours now and we think you should name him Jake." Syd smiled and added, "We're starting over, Alex, and this time we'll all make better choices." She wrapped her arm around Alex's shoulder and coaxed her to her feet.

Yolanda rounded the table and helped Alex into a long, down coat, handed her some gloves and slapped a hat on her head. The loving, safe human contact was overwhelming and Alex fought back tears, then, grinned foolishly.

Alex hugged Bertha, gently wrapped the kitten and carrier inside her coat and the foursome pushed through the doors into a swirling snowstorm. Extraordinary sunlight was creeping through the black, snow-laden clouds in radiant beams that illuminated a path right to their car.

"Now, there's a sign if I've ever seen one." Jane's mouth hung in astonishment. They all stared at the rainbow of colors dancing through the snowflakes. "It looks like God is finally showing us the right direction."

"You think he can get us through rush hour in a hurry?" Yolanda joked.

Alex slowly inhaled the fresh crisp air, closed her eyes and opened her mouth. She let the snow melt on her tongue, cheeks, eyelashes and tears. A beautiful cardinal sang a song from its homely barbed wire perch. She watched the bird flutter away, frightened to flight, as the heavy gate clanged to a close behind her.

"I believe He's been with us all along and there is no rush," smiled Alex, "If I could choose to be anywhere it would be right here, with everyone I love, on the safe side of that gate. I'm exactly where I want to be."

LaVergne, TN USA
17 January 2011
212667LV00001B/97/P